MW01260223

The World As It Should Be

Lee Ann Kostempski

MOCHA MEMOIRS PRESS

Copyright Notice

The story contained therein are works of fiction. Names, characters, places, and incidents are products of the authors' imagination or are used fictitiously and are not to be construed as real. Any resemblance to actual events, locales, organizations, or persons, living or dead, is entirely coincidental.

ISBN: 978-1-962353-00-7

Copyright©2022 Lee Ann Kostempski

Cover Art by Maya Preisler

Editor: Rie Sheridan Rose

Proofreader: Nicole Givens Kurtz

Publisher: Mocha Memoirs Press

All rights reserved. No part of this book may be used or reproduced electronically or in print without written permission, except in the case of brief quotations embodied in reviews. Due to copyright laws you cannot trade, sell or give any e-books away.

Other Mocha Memoirs Horror titles

Blackened Roots: An Anthology of the Undead edited by Tonia Ransom and Nicole Givens Kurtz

SLAY: Stories of the Vampire Noire edited by Nicole Givens Kurtz

Black Magic Women edited by Sumiko Saulson

In the Bloodstream: An Anthology of Dark Fantasy and Horror edited by Eden Royce

Sisters of the Wild Sage: A Weird Western Collection by Nicole Givens Kurtz

Ghosts, Gears, and Grimoires edited by Rie Sheridan Rose

Chapter One

Charity Olmstead trudged along the bank of the Crane River, collecting the heaviest stones she could find and tucking them into her jacket pockets. Her bare, blistered, bloody feet ached. She'd been wandering the ruins of Salem for forty-eight hours straight, and now she wanted nothing more than to die.

Stupid of her to think there was ever any hope. She'd wanted to believe so badly there was a bright side to the end of the world. No more tyrannical governments. No more eighty-hour work weeks. No more doom-scrolling through all the bad news alerts on her phone: looming wars, economic collapse, climate disasters, one right after another after another after another. She'd been on autopilot, crawling from paycheck to paycheck for so long she'd forgotten what it felt like to live.

When the apocalypse finally arrived and the horrors of that night faded, Charity briefly remembered the taste of happiness. For perhaps the first time in her life, she was one of the lucky ones. A survivor. The earthquakes and the dragon-fire somehow skipped right past her tiny, over-priced studio apartment. Her cupboards were well-stocked with non-perishables; after a month and a half holed up in her sanctuary, she still hadn't run out of food. She no longer had to worry about working three jobs to make rent—there was no rent! Best of all, there was no more news.

In that fleeting month and a half, she knew freedom for the first time in nearly ten years.

Then, two nights ago, Dean had shown up on her doorstep, wounded and weeping. How could she resist? She let him in, gave him some painkillers and fresh bandages for the hand he cradled against his chest. He apologized for the way things had ended between them, swore he was a changed man.

He kissed her.

And even now—after everything he'd taken from her—she still believed in that kiss. It had tasted like truth.

Pity she would never learn what that meant for them.

Once her guard was down, Dean had held a gun to her head. Said he needed the apartment for himself and his mother, Nora. When Charity asked why she couldn't just live with them, all he said was, "Get out of Salem, Cher. Fast."

He didn't even have the decency to let her put on any shoes first. He just grabbed her red leather jacket from the coat rack, shoved it into her arms, and slammed the door in her face so hard she thought for a second he'd fired the gun.

And now, after two long days spent trying and failing to forage for food, hiding from wildlife and ghosts, and searching without luck for any shelter or other survivors, Charity stared into the Crane River and prepared to die.

She would rather kill herself than go back to living in survival mode.

She'd been living on borrowed time anyway; her rations would have run out eventually, and then what? Dean had only sped up the process.

Something broke the moon's reflection in the middle of the river, a tiny bobbing light. It drew nearer to the bank until it reached the shallows, then a creature rose up beneath it.

Charity took great pride in her knowledge of magic and fairy tales, being the daughter of Salem's most famous psychic duo. She knew without a doubt the thing in the river was a kelpie.

Except it didn't look like the one in the illustrations from the big, gold-edged pages of the books her parents used to read to her when she was little. *Those* kelpies were always beautiful blue-black horses, seaweed tangled in their thick manes. The most terrifying physical traits they possessed were their glowing eyes, though that wasn't really anything to be afraid of—if you had asked little Cher's opinion. She'd thought they were kind of cool, actually.

The thing standing before her now was shaped, for the most part, like a horse.

But it was far from beautiful.

Its coat was not dark and velvety, but the gross pink-ish-white of a fish's underbelly, and its skin clung to its bones like heavy, soaking laundry hung out to dry. It had the permanently bared teeth of an anglerfish, too long even for its enormous horse jaw. On its forehead was the bobbing light, the *esca*, meant to hypnotize its prey with its enchanting glow. Its nose was stunted, the skin of its face decaying and exposing the bone underneath, and its black mane was scraggly and short-cropped, like the hair of a drowned corpse that had served as a snack for tadpoles.

The eyes were the worst part. They were not the eyes of a horse, nor the cool blue eyes of the kelpies in Cher's old books, nor even the milky eyes of a deep-sea fish. No, they were distinctly human—and lidless. Small, round pupils, with small, round irises to match, too small for its disproportionately huge, bloodshot eyeballs.

Those eyes were fixed on Cher. Yet she wasn't afraid.

"You aren't going to run away screaming?" the creature asked her.

He did not speak aloud, but rather projected his voice into Cher's mind. It was a soothing voice, deep and rolling like the river's current.

She smiled sadly. "No offense," she said—aloud, because it was the only way she knew how to talk—"but I'm too tired to be scared anymore."

"Fair enough."

"I'm sure anyone else would be terrified of you, though."

"So kind of you to say." The kelpie held his head tall and proud. "What brings you to the Crane River?"

With both hands, she reached into her jacket pockets to show him some of the stones.

"Ah," said the kelpie, flattening his ears humbly; like his mane, they had been nibbled down to stubs by the river's inhabitants. "Rough day?"

"Yeah," Cher sighed. "Rough decade, really."

"I see. I'm sorry."

"It's not your fault." She shrugged and tucked the

stones back into her pockets, chewing at a nail as she watched the kelpie lap up a mouthful of water.

If she stepped into the water now, she wondered, would the kelpie wait to eat her until she was dead? Or did he prefer his meals alive? He wasn't quite as feral as she'd always imagined a kelpie would be, but he was still a wild creature, and a carnivore at that. He had to eat.

So why wasn't he casting his spell and luring her into the river, like all the stories warned he would? Was he only waiting for her to do all the work and take her own life?

"Hey," she said, and cleared her throat. "Listen. I would rather.... I mean, could you do me a favor?"

"I already know what you're going to ask," said the kelpie. "The answer is no."

Cher bristled, indignant. "How could you possibly know?" she asked.

"I know everything about every human I meet. If I couldn't read your souls like books, I wouldn't be able to shape-shift into your hearts' desires and lure you to your watery deaths." The creature attempted something like a patient smile. A glob of drool dripped from between his teeth and fell with a plop into the river. "Besides, it doesn't take a psychic to know you want me to ease your death. What else am I good for?"

She ceded that point to him. "Well, why won't you do it then?"

"Because I just ate a little while ago," he explained. "Quite a large human. I'm stuffed. If I ate you now, I would only upset my delicate bowels."

Cher plopped down on the bank, letting the river soak her aching feet. "I'll wait then," she said. "Until you're ready to eat again."

5

The kelpie shifted his weight. "I do hate to let a willing meal walk away," he muttered. "But it may be a while before I'm hungry again. We kelpies are very efficient at storing nutrients away. Like alligators." He clacked his teeth together.

"How often do you eat?"

"Oh, hmm, about every two weeks. I suppose if I don't snack on any fish, I might want a full meal again in one."

Cher withered. "I guess I don't mind waiting that long," she said, though she did mind very much. She just wanted to get it over with.

The kelpie huffed a breath of air through his rotting nostrils. He didn't say anything for many moments, only watched as Cher took the stones from her pockets one by one and stacked them in a small pile in the dirt.

"I don't think you mean it," he said eventually.

Cher closed her fingers around the stone in her palm and frowned at him. "Of course I do."

"No, you don't," said the kelpie. "I can see into your soul, remember? You do not want me to eat you."

Frowning deeper, Cher probed her own heart for something she wanted more than blissful eternal rest. She shook her head and replied, "I can't imagine a better way to go, except maybe passing away in my sleep. I assume the way your magic works is something like that, right? I wouldn't be aware I was dying. Whatever dream you offer to me would overpower reality."

"That is correct," the kelpie said, "but that isn't what I mean. You don't want to die at all."

She laughed so hard she almost snorted. "I think I know my own soul better than you do."

"I doubt that. But, ah—why don't you come back next week and we'll see who's right?"

Cher found the kelpie's condescension infuriating, but what a fascinating creature he was. She watched as he waded back into the center of the river and opened the gills on his neck before diving into the current. When he resurfaced, the gills sealed shut again and he shook the water from his mane.

"You're still here?" he said when he spotted her sitting on the bank.

"It's not like I have anywhere else to be." She pulled her knees up to her chest and rested her chin upon them, plucking a blade of grass from the ground and peeling it in half.

"It'll be an awfully long week waiting for my appetite to return if all you're going to do is sit there," said the kelpie. He tilted his head to one side. "I could use the company though, I suppose. My little one recently ventured off to find an estuary of his own, and now I'm all by my lonesome."

"Do you have a mate?" Cher asked.

"I did. She was killed by some humans. Monster hunters, by the looks of them, all decked out in weaponry." He shuddered.

"Oh. I'm so sorry."

"Thank you." He stared into the water, apparently lost in thought. Then the light on his forehead brightened. "How about you do me a favor? It will pass the time until I'm ready to eat again."

"It's not enough I'm saving you a hunt? I'm practically serving myself to you on a silver platter."

"That *is* considerate of you. But there's something else I

want. Something I'm hungry for. And I think you can help me."

Cher leaned back, her palms pressed against the rocky riverbank. "Is it revenge?"

"For my mate, yes." The kelpie whinnied softly, like a laugh. "Goodness, you saw my own desire so plainly. We aren't usually a cannibalistic species, but now I'm wondering whether you're a kelpie too, here to lure me to my own death."

"Nope. I only made an educated guess," she said, shrugging. "If I were you, I'd want revenge too. But what makes you think I can help?"

"I'll show you. Just remember—I know you better than you know yourself. You'll see."

"What's that supposed to mean?"

But the kelpie didn't answer. Instead he closed the distance between them, water sluicing off his flanks as he stepped out of the river and onto dry land.

Cher climbed hesitantly to her feet to greet him. He smelled so potently of mildew and mold she pinched her nose shut.

"You'll get used to it," he said. "Now, up-up."

"Is this a trick? Are you hungry after all?"

"No," the kelpie answered simply and honestly. A saddle appeared on his back, materializing from the water droplets that dripped from his skin. It was made of a black, polished leather with a glittering diamond orb embedded in the tip of the horn.

"I'd be stupid to trust you."

"Maybe so. But what do you care? I thought you wanted to die."

"I do."

She placed her foot in the stirrup and swung up into the saddle with a stubborn huff.

Yet, as the kelpie started trotting at a leisurely pace, Cher's chest felt suddenly tight. Was that anxiety gripping her lungs in a vise, or was it the rushing river suffocating her? She could be drowning right now, even as they walked away from the Crane River, and she wouldn't even know it.

"Stop that," the kelpie chided her. "What a boring twist that would be. You can relax for now. I assure you this is no illusion." He paused, then added, "But in the end, I'm going to eat you whether or not you recognize your heart's true desire and change your mind about dying. A deal is a deal, Charity Olmstead. You promised me a meal."

Something pricked Cher's left palm as she rested it on the saddle horn. With a soft gasp, she yanked her hand back and looked down to see a ring of needles like a lamprey's mouth sinking back into the diamond, staining the crystal red with her blood.

The kelpie shivered with delight and said, "I look forward to fulfilling the terms of our contract."

Chapter Two

"So," said Charity, absentmindedly examining the wound on her palm and tracing the perfect circle of bloody dots. "What's your name? You know mine and, if we have a contract, then I think it's only fair I know yours too."

"I don't have one," said the kelpie as he steered them south. "A name is too permanent, too constricting. Like a bridle. We kelpies prefer to be free as flowing water."

Okay, Shakespeare, no need to get all poetic, Cher thought, rolling her eyes behind his back. Maybe spending a week with him would be too unbearable after all.

"My name is not Shakespeare," the kelpie said. "I just told you I have no name."

She'd forgotten he could read minds.

"I was being sarcastic."

His ribs heaved beneath her with a sigh. "I know," he said. "So was I. Keep up, Charity Olmstead."

God, you're annoying.

He reared without warning. Cher shrieked and hugged

his neck, clinging desperately as he kicked his front legs in the air. He landed again with a heavy thud that nearly jolted her out of the saddle.

"Oh, sorry," he said, in a tone implying he wasn't sorry at all.

They wandered further inland, and Cher was glad the kelpie seemed to know where he was going. Salem was unrecognizable to her. Thousands of magically-grown trees had reshaped the entire horizon, and the scents of freshly-churned earth and rotting bodies masked its familiar sea-salt smell. All traces of civilization were either hidden underneath creeping vines and crushing roots or gone completely. The land had rearranged itself, new hills springing up where there were once paved streets, parks bursting into woods, and then into a full forest.

What remained of Salem looked as though it had been abandoned for a century at least, not for only two months.

Though perhaps "abandoned" was the wrong word for it. The dead hadn't actually left Salem at all. They still roamed the streets, watching silently as the kelpie weaved his way among them. Their faintly glowing eyes, full of agony, always lingered on Cher as if they knew who her parents were. As if they hoped she could help them, the same way Theodore and Roslyn Olmstead used to help the dead find peace.

But she couldn't. She had no clue how to deal with ghosts. And, frankly, she didn't have the emotional energy to learn. Maybe once upon a time she would have, when she was young and eager and not yet crushed by the world.

She took care now to look through the dead, or over their heads, pretending not to see them, pretending not to feel their gazes on her as she looked instead for some landmark that might tell her where exactly in Salem they were going.

After losing her apartment to Dean, Cher had tried making her way east to the Atlantic Ocean. She hoped she might find a boat so she could sail away and look for help in another city.

Instead, she somehow ended up just about everywhere but the coast. The Crane River had been a welcome sight when she finally stumbled upon it, but by then her will to live had left her again.

"What were you doing when the world renewed itself?" the kelpie asked her, breaking the silence.

"*Renewed itself*? That's an interesting way to put it."

"What would you call it? An ending?" the kelpie asked, and Cher hummed affirmatively. "It didn't end though, technically speaking. It's still here. You're still here. Everything's changed, is all."

"I guess you're right." She shrugged. "I was washing dishes."

She'd been putting those dishes off for weeks. Who had time for cleaning when they came home from one job and had less than three hours to sleep before they'd wake up to the blaring alarm for their next job? Anyway, she'd been ordering takeout more and more so she could carve cooking and lunch prep out of her hectic schedule. She'd been eating straight out of Styrofoam containers, so clean dishes were a low priority.

The night before the end of the world was the first she'd had off in ages. She'd finally gone grocery shopping, and she was looking forward to cooking some spaghetti and meatballs. Real food, not fast food.

"And what were you thinking of while you were doing that?" the kelpie said. "Did you make any wishes?"

She tensed. "You already know the answer to that." He could read her mind; why should she tell him all this?

"I'm trying to make a point here."

"Fine. I'll play along."

Cher remembered that night in vivid detail: the full moon shining in through the kitchen window, so weirdly bright she didn't bother turning on the lights; the glow of the TV screen across from the open kitchen, and the offensively orange tie of the news anchor; the steak knife slicing through the sponge and cutting her thumb, so deep it had since scarred.

Instead of getting a bandage, she'd watched the blood pool and then drip down her thumb, into the sink.

"I wished for an easy way out," she said to the kelpie. "I just thought, what a relief it would be to—to take that blade..." She paused, swallowed hard.

"What's wrong, Charity Olmstead?" There was tenderness in the kelpie's tone.

"That darkness just crept up on me. So suddenly." She frowned. "It must've been lurking for a long time. Growing."

She had lost so much in a decade. First all of her friends, then her dream job, her parents, a girlfriend, a fiancé, her freedom. She was so lonely by the end. Relationships took time, but so did making ends meet in President Bates' crumbling capitalist hellscape. She couldn't do both.

"Anyway," she said, "what's the point you're trying to make?"

"You wished for an easy way out, and you received one.

13

When the world changed, you were freed from the life you resented. Don't you want to seize that opportunity?"

"I appreciate the fact you're trying to shift my perspective," Cher said. "But it isn't that simple. The old stresses are gone, sure. But there are new ones."

She pointed to a pile of charred bodies beside the path, which she tried very hard not to look at directly.

"That," she said. "That was traumatizing. I covered my ears, but I could still hear everyone screaming. Buildings exploding. Howling wind. Dragons and other monsters roaring."

"Fair."

"The world is still ugly and cruel and terrifying. And I remain convinced there's no place for me in it."

"Mm. We'll see."

Cher's frown deepened as she spotted a toppled gas station sign, rusted and crumpling under the weight of some rubble. They were strolling down a grassy path that was once a street.

Her street.

The same second she recognized the neighborhood, the kelpie sensed the shift in her mood and picked up his pace to a canter.

"Why are we here?" she asked, bewildered. "Turn around. Dean will kill me." Or at least he'd implied he would if she set foot anywhere near the apartment again.

Yet she couldn't stop thinking about how he'd warned her to get out of Salem, as if he wanted to protect her from something. What did he know?

Plus, there was that damned kiss. She wanted to believe he wouldn't harm her, not after that. He still loved her too much. Didn't he?

She didn't want to test that theory.

"I thought you wanted to die," the kelpie said once more, no less condescending.

"I do," she assured him again, "but not by Dean's hand." It would be one of the worst ways to go, suffering heartbreak as she bled out from a bullet wound.

"My, you are a picky one. *Tsk*."

Cher ducked down in the saddle, bracing herself for the gunshot. Maybe if she buried her face in the kelpie's slimy mane Dean wouldn't recognize her.

"Please turn around," she begged. "He'll kill you too." Her voice, already shaky with fear, bounced in her chest with every *clump* of the kelpie's hooves in the dirt.

"I dare him to try," he said, growling deep within his chest. "There's no need to worry though. Dean Winston is not here." He slowed to a halt.

Cher's knuckles were white around the saddle horn. "Then his mother—"

"Nora isn't here either. Look up, Charity Olmstead."

She did.

The first thing she saw was the giant hawthorn tree. It hadn't been there two months ago. The night of the apocalypse, it burst up out of the front lawn of the apartment complex, its branches knocking down a streetlamp and punching out windows—including the one in Cher's second-floor unit.

The tree looked even larger now. So large, in fact, she didn't notice right away that the building behind it was gone.

"Where is it?"

The kelpie flicked his tail toward a mound of bricks

and wooden beams behind the tree. "It collapsed," he said with glee.

Cher made no reply, only slipped off his back and rounded the thick tree trunk to get a better look at what was left of her apartment.

All her belongings, all of her memories were trapped somewhere under that wreckage. The last photographs of her parents. Her precious fairy tale books. The thought made her heart ache.

Her rent had been way too high, utilities were not included, and her landlord charged for washing machine use on top of that. But it was the cheapest she could find in Salem, and she'd grown to love the apartment over the six years she'd called it home.

"Dean...?" she wondered aloud, turning back to face the kelpie.

"He made it out alive," he said, coming to stand by her side. "So did his mother. Unfortunately."

"How do you know?"

"The real question is, why do you care either way? He took this away from you. Do you not hate him? Are you not glad karma intervened? Isn't that what you wanted?"

The next words that sounded in Cher's head weren't the kelpie's, they were her own—a memory of her parting words to Dean, forced upon her now by the kelpie's magic:

"Fuck you," she'd yelled at him through the door after he slammed it in her face.

Her parents had blessed the apartment for her when she moved into it; she believed now it was because of their blessing the apartment had withstood the apocalypse. How dare Dean take that from her? It was all she had left. If this was how he was going to be, she wouldn't let him benefit from her parents' protective love.

Let the place burn.

"Fuck you!" she screamed again, with all the fury of a witch casting a curse as she pounded her fist against the door. "You're a monster—"

"Stop." Cher shut her eyes against the memories and turned her face away from the kelpie so he would not see her tears.

"Did you really believe, even for one second, he had changed?" he said, not unkindly, yet Cher's fingers still curled into fists. "He's the same man you left years ago. Blindly loyal to his mother and father. Remind me—what was it he said to you, the night you left him? When you begged him to turn in his badge?"

Again the kelpie's voice changed, this time to Dean's: "*I was just following orders.*"

"You and I both know," the kelpie said, "that is no excuse. And yet, he did it again. To *you* this time! His mother commanded him to kick you out and he was only too eager to please her; the same way he jumped to obey his father when he ordered him to fire on those protesters—"

"I said stop."

It was bad enough being reminded of such painful conversations with someone she once considered the love of her life. The way the kelpie accessed those moments, sifting through her mind, was only salt in the wound. So invasive. So violating. She wrapped her arms around herself.

The kelpie sighed. "Yes, well, I see that's still a sore subject. My apologies." For once he sounded genuine, at least. "I was only trying to help you turn your grief into some good old-fashioned, self-righteous anger. It feels much better that way. But I guess you aren't ready for that stage yet." He flattened his gnarled ears against his skull. "Congratulations anyway. You do know what this means, don't you?"

When she only stared blankly at him, he tilted his head in the direction of the apartment ruins and said, "This is your doing."

"*Mine?*"

"You are an Olmstead. Your parents were both powerful witches, yes?"

She nodded.

"This is how you can help me," said the kelpie. "Those who killed my mate...I believe they may be under the influence of some old, twisted spirits. There were ghosts on the shore, watching the humans murder her. Like they were supervising them. And smiling all the while."

Cher shivered and kept her eyes glued to him, trying not to see the spirits drifting all around them.

"But my powers have no effect on the dead," he continued. "I don't know why the ghosts were there, or what part they played in all this, but I know they have something to do with it. Perhaps—perhaps the humans are trying to drive monsters like me to extinction. I don't know why the ghosts would help, or...I don't know." He tilted his head thoughtfully, then shook it as if to clear his mind. "Anyhow, if you master your abilities, I believe we can stop them. Both the living and the dead."

Cher's eyes widened. "Oh, no," she said, backing away from him, "no, thank you. I never agreed to *this*." She gestured at their surroundings and noticed her hands shook. "I don't want the power to curse someone or kill them. I don't want to see the dead."

The kelpie stamped a hoof into the earth and rounded on her, baring his teeth in a snarl. She had let her guard down; his abrupt transformation struck fear into her veins.

"You have no choice," he growled, forcing her back against the hawthorn tree. "We made a deal."

Her palm tingled at this reminder. "What are you going to do if I refuse?" she said, lifting her chin in defiance. "Kill me? Then you'll only be giving me exactly what I want."

"Oh, I'll kill you," the kelpie said, creeping closer to her, "but I won't make it nice. First I will flood your mind with horrors you cannot even fathom."

An image flashed across her mind: she was under dark, murky water and an enormous set of teeth loomed at her from the shadows.

"Then," said the kelpie, "I will make sure you live long enough to feel my jaws crush every bone in your body."

He didn't simulate the pain with his spell, but he made sure she heard skin and bone being ripped to shreds.

Once Cher was appropriately cowed, he softened his tone to a more clipped, business-like one. "I cannot take revenge alone, and I need more than a mere human's help. I need a witch. And not just any witch, but the daughter of Salem's most powerful psychics."

"But I don't know the first thing about magic," Cher replied, her voice small and frightened. What had she gotten herself into?

"Nothing to worry about." The kelpie turned away from her and flicked his tail. "I know someone who can teach you. Come now. Up-up."

Chapter Three

Disenchanted with the quest after their argument, Cher brooded herself to sleep in the saddle. She slumped forward, arms hanging loosely around the kelpie's neck, cheek pressed against the back of his broad neck.

He walked slowly to protect her from falling; she would be of no use to him with a concussion, after all. He needed her as healthy and strong as she could be. Which meant letting her sleep—and finding her food and drink.

After some time spent wandering along the shore of the North River, they came to a spot where it narrowed into a stream. On the bank stood a grand willow tree with a soft pile of clover growing beneath it. The kelpie shook his head, jostling his companion—or his *prey*, he reminded himself—awake.

"Charity," he said. She groaned and sat up. "You can keep sleeping. Just get down and stay here until I return."

She slid off his back and curled up beneath the tree's

curtain of branches. "Where are you going?" she asked groggily, rubbing her eyes.

"To find you some food. Get some rest. I'll return shortly."

She was half-asleep again before he even finished speaking.

He waded into the stream and swam against the current, over sunken rusty cars and a short bridge that had collapsed at the end of the world, toward the deeper estuary.

Whether Charity liked fish or not, it was the best he could bring to her. The only other food he could offer was a human being, if one happened to stumble past, but something told him Charity would not like that at all.

He came to a standstill in the center of the estuary and let his light shine. Then he waited. And waited some more. So patient. Perfectly still, except for the esca on his forehead twitching back and forth.

It was a poor yellow perch that fell for the trap.

Careful not to swallow it himself, the kelpie merely opened his jaws and speared the fish on a tooth as it danced underneath his light. It was a good, juicy catch.

Confident Charity would be grateful to him, he returned to shore with the dead fish dangling from his teeth.

She still slept, snoring softly in the patch of clover. There were goosebumps on her bare legs; all she wore beneath that red leather jacket was a periwinkle blue nightgown.

Dean Winston truly is a prick, the kelpie thought as he lowered his head to the earth and shook the fish off his tooth. It fell with a bloody *plop* next to Charity's head, but she slept on, oblivious.

When he lifted his head again, the kelpie froze. Between the wispy tree branches, a little girl in a bonnet stood staring at him.

She wore a look he knew well: that of a monster on the prowl for its next meal.

He recognized her as one of the ghosts that had watched the humans kill his mate like it was some thrilling sport.

"Oh," the little girl muttered to herself, as if thinking aloud, "did we get the wrong one?"

The kelpie gave a warning growl.

"You!" he said, stalking toward the child. She stood her ground, unwavering, even as he circled her like a prowling panther. "You were there. You *laughed* as they tore her apart. What are you doing here?"

His tone turned frantic, pupils widening as the girl smiled and he realized the truth: they must be after his spawn.

"No!" he said. "Begone! You will not bring them here. You will not take my colt too." He released a terrible, high-pitched screech, the sort of sound that had no business coming from any earthly creature, and galloped straight at the ghost.

She vanished, her laugh lingering in the air around him.

The wrong one.' What had she meant by that?

"What's happening?" Charity's hands were over her ears, her eyes wide open; his scream must have startled her awake.

"Nothing to worry about," he said, though his heart

pounded against his ribs and his eyes darted back and forth, expecting the ghost to reappear at any second. He trotted to Charity's side. "Everything is fine. I just chased off another predator who came sniffing after my prey. We can't have any of that." He nudged her a little more roughly than he intended. "Let's go. Up-up."

They needed to leave. Quickly. He knew the commotion he'd made would attract a certain someone's attention, and he couldn't have Charity around when that certain someone arrived.

"Hang on," she said. "Now you're freaking me out. What was it you chased off?"

"Just a ghost."

"A *ghost*? After *me*?"

"Probably." A half-lie. "Psychics do tend to attract the dead. You're easy targets for possession." That was a whole truth.

He should never have brought Charity here, so close to his spawn's territory. He'd led the ghost here. If anything happened to his colt now, it would be his fault.

"Possession?" Charity said, with a sarcastic grin. She was only masking her terror behind a false, exaggerated cheer. "Boy howdy, do I hate the sound of that!" She gave a shaky laugh and buried her face in her hands.

"If we find the witch I'm looking for, she can teach you how to protect yourself," he said and nosed at her again. "Come on. Are you hungry? I caught you something. You can eat while you ride."

Charity finally noticed the dead fish beside her and turned pale. "Oh, gross," she said, covering her mouth as she gagged.

"You don't like fish?"

"I like them already gutted and cooked for me. I really do not like it when they still have their eyes."

"'*Cooked*?'"

She dragged her hands down her face. "Okay. Look," she said, "I appreciate you taking care of me, I guess. Though I assume it's because you want me nice and plump when you're finally ready to eat."

The kelpie did not deny that. She didn't expect him to. "But I can't eat a raw fish," she said. "I'd get sick."

"Ah. Of course. I wasn't thinking. Never mind then. We should get a move on anyway. Hurry now, on your feet—"

"Alright, jeez." She stood. "What's the rush?"

Before he could come up with some excuse, a voice sounded behind him. "Sire?"

Damn.

The kelpie turned and saw another of his kind standing in the water. The colt was smaller, his flesh more pink than white. He had his mother's silver mane.

"It *is* you!" the colt neighed happily as he climbed ashore and nuzzled his decaying nose against his sire's. "I heard a commotion and wondered who was in my territory. What are you doing here?" He sniffed the air and frowned as his stomach rumbled. "I smell human."

The sire shielded Charity from the second kelpie's view. "*Stay*," he barked into her thoughts, adding a dash of his mind-controlling magic to the command. "*Hush.*"

He felt oddly guilty placing her under a spell. Nevertheless, he assured himself it was for her own good.

Then he turned to the other kelpie. "How are you, little one?" he asked.

"Hungry," the colt said.

"Settled into your new home well, I take it?"

"Oh, I don't know yet. It's alright, but a little too shady. Care to hunt with me, for old times' sake? That human is so close, I can taste it already."

"Ah. I would love to but, you see, I'm—in the middle of something—an important thing—"

He tried and failed to block the colt from stepping past him.

In the split second that followed, as the colt spotted Charity and salivated, the elder kelpie's heart broke. He was left with no choice.

He snapped.

The colt reared up and kicked his front hooves, just missing his sire. As he fell back down to all fours, the elder kelpie nipped at his darling little one's face and drove him back towards the stream. The colt answered with the same aggressive shriek his sire had made at the ghost just moments ago, baring all his thick, razor-sharp teeth.

"What the hell has gotten into you, Sire?" he yowled. "Are you a kelpie or not? You would deprive your own family of food? I have yet to see a single other human pass through here. I'm so hungry for a full meal, my belly aches."

"I'm sorry," the older kelpie said. "But you cannot have this one. She's doing me a favor. Doing both of us a favor."

The colt grunted. "A human?" he scoffed. "As if one of them would help the likes of us. It would kill you first."

He ignored his little one's disdain, telling him softly, "This one's a witch. We made a deal. She's had enough of life. So I've promised to give her a peaceful death, as long as she helps me avenge your dam first."

The smaller kelpie softened. "Not this again. Just let it go."

"No. I'm not just doing this for revenge. I'm doing it to protect you."

"I can look out for myself. Please, for my sake, let it go."

"There was something strange about the way those humans killed her," the sire said, brushing the colt's concern aside. "It wasn't self-defense. She wasn't even hunting, yet they targeted her. Why?"

"They probably knew someone she ate," the colt said gently. "They hate us, Sire. They hate us for our very nature. They don't need any other reason to kill us."

"But that doesn't explain what those ghosts were doing there. You saw them too."

"I assumed they were the souls of the ones the hunters wanted to avenge."

"No. Those souls felt so—*ancient*. They aren't like recent spirits. I don't trust them." He shook his head. "You need to be careful. One of them was lurking around this estuary just now." *And I might have led her here,* he thought. *I'm sorry. I'm sorry.* "I don't think they're done with us."

That gave the colt pause. "That's why you were up here screaming bloody murder."

The sire nodded. "There's something strange afoot in Salem," he said. "And it cost us your dam's life. The least I can do for her—for all of us—is find out why she had to die."

He turned his back then, leaving his spawn standing on the bank of the stream. With a simple thought, he silently commanded the still-hypnotized Charity up into his saddle.

"Find a mate, dear," he said over his shoulder to the colt. "Please. I will feel much better if you have someone watching your back. There's another kelpie downstream, you know. I think he is still unpaired."

The colt's lidless eyes rolled in their sockets.

"Of course, if you want to have a spawn of your own, one of you will need to undergo the Shift—"

"Sire."

"But that's nothing to be afraid of. Sometimes your dam and I Shifted just for fun, and—"

"*Sire!*"

"Ahem. Yes. Well. It shouldn't take me more than a week to get to the bottom of this. Stay safe until then. When this is all over, I'll bring the witch back here and we can share a meal. I promise."

"If you don't get killed first," the colt said. "And if I don't starve before then."

His words were a whip against the sire's hindquarters. "I will not let that happen," the kelpie promised, hooves kicking up dirt as he galloped away from the estuary.

Chapter Four

When they were a safe distance away, the kelpie severed the power he held over Cher. She blinked and yawned as if she'd only just awoken from her nap beneath the willow tree.

"What happened?" she asked.

"We ran into another predator," the kelpie said. He didn't mention it was his own colt; the wounds of their argument were still too fresh. "I did what I had to do to protect you and placed you under a spell. My apologies."

He expected outrage, but Cher only shrugged it off. "I dreamed you were a unicorn instead of a kelpie," she said. "You let me brush your mane and weave pink and purple flowers into it."

"Sounds more like a nightmare."

"I enjoyed it."

She wasn't happy to be awake again. Somewhere in the back of her mind, as she'd braided the unicorn's mane, she'd suspected it was a dream. *The* dream, the one the kelpie had promised to give her while he drowned her in the real world. She'd thought to herself, *See, this isn't such a bad way to go.*

Now she was back here, more aware than ever of the kelpie's mildew stench as he steered them around dozens and dozens of the dead.

"Don't you think they're horrifying?" she said. "The ghosts?"

"You're frightened of *them*, but not *me*?" The kelpie nearly tripped over his own hooves, he was so taken aback. "What happened to being too numb for fear?"

"I'm sorry, did I bruise your ego?" She tugged a strand of his mane and laughed.

But her joy was short-lived. The kelpie stepped right through a crowd of spirits, dousing Cher in an icy cloud. Her heartbeat raced and a cold sweat trickled down the back of her neck.

"You really *are* terrified of them," the kelpie said. "Amazing."

"Yeah. Well, if I make eye contact with any of them, I relive the end of the world over and over and over again, from a different victim's perspective every single time."

She'd learned that the hard way her first night in the wilderness. It was so overwhelming that she'd cowered under a tree, curled up in a tight ball after accidentally locking eyes with just one ghost.

The poor child's death was so vivid she felt the sensation of her own skin burning; of her own skull crushed under falling bricks.

Every time she peeked out from between her fingers, she'd find another ghost crouching in front of her, curious about the psychic having a breakdown. And if she made the mistake of eye contact, she saw more, felt more: limbs being torn off, tree roots breaking ribs, hearts literally ripped from chests.

"But you..." she said to the kelpie thoughtfully, shaking the memories away. "For one thing, you're a new species to me, at least in real life. So that instantly makes you interesting. I studied zoology in school, y'know. Got to be a zookeeper for about six months. That is, before Bates cut funding and all the zoos in America were shut down."

"I'm going to pretend I know what any of that means."

Cher ignored him, continuing, "Sure, you're hideous. I'll grant you that—"

"Thank you."

"—but I think you're just a big ol' softy, deep down."

He whipped his tail. "I resent that."

She laughed. *Laughed!* At the mighty kelpie! He nearly devoured her on the spot. Had she already forgotten the threats he'd made to her?

"You claim to know more about me than I know myself," she said. "Well, maybe the reverse is true too. You ever think of that?"

"That's enough," he warned her, and the tone of his command was enough to shut her up—a not-so-friendly reminder of their argument outside the ruins of her apartment. "Best not get comfortable, Charity Olmstead. Don't forget, I am a monster after all."

He tried taking comfort from the uneasy silence that followed, the little boost to his dignity as he reestablished the pecking order. But all he could think of was the disgust in his colt's tone.

Are you a kelpie or not?

His little one was right; he should be ashamed to cart this human around Salem, to laugh with her and treat her like kin, to pity her and bond with her and hope she would find something worth living for. It was his nature to kill humans, not befriend them, just as it was human nature to kill monsters like him. Rage churned in his belly when he thought of how demeaning all of this was, and the temptation to turn around and present Charity to his colt nearly overpowered him, deal be damned.

But then, she asked, "How will we know where to find the hunters who killed your mate?" and the kelpie remembered his vow.

If he killed Charity now—essentially breaking the terms of their contract—he would only screw himself. She would still get what she wanted, but all his questions would be left unanswered. His mate would have died in vain. He could bear losing some of his little one's respect if it meant he got his revenge.

It was only for a little while; when he got to the bottom of everything, the colt would understand why he had to do this.

"I managed to ensnare one of the hunters during the battle and lure him away from the rest," he explained. "He was just about to climb into my saddle. He had his hand on the horn, so I drew his blood the same way I drew yours. It's very rare our prey gets away from us, but in the event it does happen, storing their blood allows us to track them better."

Cher instinctively curled her fingers into a fist over the injury on her own palm. "I see."

"That one did get away, unfortunately," said the kelpie. "One of his companions, a young woman, attacked me and broke the spell. Do you see the gouge on the back of my neck?"

She looked down and noticed, for the first time, a nasty-looking, half-healed wound. It looked as though someone had scooped a chunk of his flesh off with a ladle. The skin around the edges of the thick, muddy-red scab was mangled.

"That's not anywhere near as awful as what they did to my mate," he said, slowing to a canter as the memory of that night overwhelmed him. "But it hurt like hell. Twice as bad, knowing my mate was gone. By that point, she was dead in a pool of her own blood on the bank. I retreated while I could." Grief crept into his voice. "I should have stayed and fought. I should have killed them all."

"You were outnumbered," Cher said, her voice soft and soothing. "And I'm sure your mate wouldn't have wanted you to die too." She brushed her fingers through his still-damp mane.

He stopped walking for just a moment, craning his neck up into her touch.

"Thank you," he said. "I truly believe I'm doing the right thing. And I'm grateful for your help."

"You say that like you gave me a choice," Cher said, nudging his side playfully with her knee.

"But I did!" the kelpie insisted. "Stop being so quick to forget our deal."

"I had no idea what I was getting into."

Her rebuttal was halfhearted. In truth, the thought of learning how to control her psychic abilities had already grown on her, especially if it meant she could fend off the ghosts' unwelcome attention.

"But you did agree to help me," said the kelpie.

She kneed him again, a little harder this time, and pouted. "Fine," she said, "you won this round."

The kelpie smiled to himself as he picked the pace up again. If he was stuck working with a human being, he was glad it was Charity Olmstead.

Chapter Five

B y mid-afternoon, they had reached the coast.

There were fewer bodies here—fewer ghosts along the shoreline. The night the world had ended, earthquakes and storm-winds had churned up the biggest waves Salem had ever seen. No doubt the tossing, roiling ocean had dragged most of the corpses into its depths.

Just like the kelpie will drag me away, Cher thought, gnawing on her lip.

The kelpie paused in his tireless trek, halting atop a cliff overlooking the ocean and allowing her a moment to admire the sunshine shimmering on the Atlantic's surface.

"Beautiful as ever," she said.

Movement far, far in the distance caught her eye and her heart skipped a beat. She leaned forward, digging the nails of one hand into the saddle horn and lifting the other to block the sun from her eyes.

"Are those—?"

She pointed out to sea, where something huge broke

the surface: a tail lifted and flopped down again, spraying glittering drops of water up into the air.

"Humpbacks!" She spoke breathlessly as she dropped from the saddle and ran to the cliff-side. "Oh, my God."

Another, smaller tail mimicked the first, then a third.

"Oh, my God!" Cher laughed, an unbridled laugh full of pure joy, and ran in circles before running back to the kelpie and throwing her arms around his neck. "It's a whole pod!"

He grumbled and tried to shake her off, but that only seemed to make her squeeze tighter. "What's the big deal, Charity Olmstead?" he said.

She ignored him and ran back to the cliff top, waving her arms above her head as if the whales could see her. Tears flowed freely down her cheeks, yet she carried on laughing.

As the kelpie watched her, one of her memories struck him:

"Cherbear, look," said a woman with thick, auburn-and-gray hair. Charity's mother, Roslyn Olmstead. "There, you see it?"

Someone lifted little Charity up into the air so that she could see better over the railing of the boat. Thick arms. Hairy arms.

"See the baby?" her father, Teddy, said.

She clapped her small hands together and giggled, the same sound she made now nearly thirty years later.

Then another memory:

An older Charity, adult, sitting at a table inside her apartment. Weeping as she looked at photographs from that whale-watching trip.

"They went extinct," the kelpie said as he joined her near the edge of the cliff.

She paid him no mind. She was still too busy jumping up and down, cupping her hands around her mouth and yelling, "*Welcome back! We missed you!*"

A spout of water from a whale's blowhole caught the sunlight and made a rainbow.

Cher fell abruptly to her knees and covered her face in her hands, shaking with sobs. It was too much; she couldn't remember the last time she'd been so happy.

"Hey, now. Why are you crying?"

"I just wish M-Mom and Dad were here," she wept. "I wish they could see this."

He brushed his nose against her forehead. She reached out a hand blindly, seeking the comfort of his mane.

Instead she nicked her wrist against one of his giant teeth.

Gasping, she cradled her arm against her chest. A warm spot of blood bloomed and stained her nightgown.

When she looked up she found the kelpie's wide, lidless eyes fixed on her, his jaw tight, chest heaving.

He backed away from her.

"You're not hungry," she reminded him, her voice tiny with fear. "You said you weren't—"

"I'm not a *vampire*," the kelpie snapped. "One drop of blood doesn't send me into a frenzy."

Or it didn't usually.

"Then what's wrong?"

"Nothing. I was worried I hurt you, that's all. Are you okay?" he asked her, moving back to her side.

Cher relaxed and patted his cheek. "I'm alright," she said. "It's not that bad. See?" She held up her wrist and showed him the line of blood there, so thin it was closer to pink than it was to red. "Just surprised me is all."

Her cheeks were still wet with tears. She wiped them dry and climbed to her feet, looked back out over the sea. The whales were gone.

"Well. This was nice," she sighed. "Come, now." She imitated the kelpie's voice. "Up-up. Let's go find my mentor." She swung into the saddle. "When you finally eat me, promise me you'll let me dream I'm swimming with the whales."

"Okay."

"And I want my parents to be there too."

"You know, you could just *live* in this world full of whales and magic," the kelpie pointed out. "Happily ever after. I think that's what your parents would want for you. Didn't they want you to become a witch like them?"

"They did."

"And don't you regret turning them down when they offered to teach you the craft?"

"I do."

It had been a stupid, childish, vain decision. At thirteen, all she had wanted was to fit in. Most of the other kids at school gave her a hard time about her parents' psychic business. They called them nut-jobs and con-artists; called Cher a freaky spawn of Satan.

She never told her parents. She just lied and said she wasn't interested in magic anymore when they'd asked if she wanted to begin her lessons.

What's so great about witches anyway? she'd wondered at the time, with her teenage logic. If magic was so powerful, why wasn't the world a perfect, happy place?

For more than a decade after that thirteenth birthday,

history-in-the-making only proved her theory right. Magic was useless in the face of war and corruption and economic turmoil.

But now? Now, there was no denying it. Magic was everywhere. It had turned the Earth into a living, breathing fairy tale.

Cher chewed on this thought for a while. It was a beautiful world, despite all the horror it took to make it. And there was so much more of it to explore, so many new species to study.

Yet she was afraid to get her hopes up, only to have them brutally crushed again. There was an ugliness lurking under all the new, colorful beauty. She sensed it in the way the dead whispered about her. She sensed it whenever she remembered Dean's warning: *Get out of Salem. Fast.*

"Stop being so quick to forget our deal," she said, mimicking the kelpie once more. "Even if I decided I wanted to live—which I assure you, I won't—I couldn't. You're going to eat me either way, remember?"

"I remember," he said.

He knew she was lying still. But he'd been lugging her around all day and he didn't have the energy to debate.

"Great. So, promise me you'll let me swim in the ocean with the whales and my parents."

"Alright, Charity Olmstead. I promise."

He promised, even though just the thought of tasting Charity's blood again curdled his stomach.

Chapter Six

The sun sank and the dragons rose for their nightly hunt.

One came from the sea, another from deep within the forest. The third climbed from a chasm that had split what used to be Essex Street in half, and the fourth lifted off from a range of newly-grown mountains in the distance.

The kelpie stopped his galloping and slipped into the shadows, extinguishing the light of his esca and hugging tight to the line of trees as he followed the forest north. He placed his hooves gently, careful to muffle their sound in the dirt.

"Are you afraid of them?" Charity asked him. She'd seen the beasts drifting through the skies every night since the end of the world, but they never came close to her apartment. It wasn't until now, as she watched the dragon from Essex Street swoop low to the ground a few ruined blocks away, she realized how enormous they really were.

The kelpie's whole body tensed. "I heartily respect

them," he said. "Revere them, even! They helped shape this world for us monsters after all. But they do have mighty appetites, and I assume we kelpies are just about the right size to satiate them."

He had never seen a dragon eat a kelpie, wasn't even sure they were carnivorous, but he wasn't about to find out. They were bigger than he was, and he simply did not like that.

"Oh, good!" He stopped and gestured with a toss of his head for Charity to look at the trees. "That's what we're looking for."

A bluish orb bobbed and weaved between the trunks, then flickered out.

"Fireflies?" Charity guessed. "Giant fireflies?"

"Not quite." The kelpie stepped into the forest and instantly relaxed under the cover of its canopy. "Will-o-the-wisps." Several more of the lights flickered around them, dazzlingly bright in the pitch black.

Charity threw an arm up over her eyes as one of the wisps flashed right at the tip of her nose. "Uh, don't these things usually lure travelers to their swampy deaths?" she asked.

The kelpie gave a wheezy laugh.

"That's *my* job," he said. "My guess is whatever dumb human wrote your fairy tales mixed up kelpies and wisps. Which is understandable, I suppose, given the truth."

He reignited his esca. It looked like a wisp, right down to its bluish tint.

"Will-o-the-wisps *actually* light the safest path through swamps," he explained. "There are some kelpies who prefer to live in bogs, and it is their esca that lure humans into the water. Some say bogs were actually our original biome, many thousands of years ago."

He snapped his teeth at one of the nearby wisps, chasing it away from his face.

Cher wished she had a notebook to write down every word he said. "Fascinating," she whispered.

"There's no confirmation whether it's true or not," the kelpie said. "For all we know, we might be a cross between a seahorse and an anglerfish, which gradually evolved into something more like a land-horse. Don't ask me how. Science is a magic of its own kind, one far beyond even my vast knowledge."

"Have you always been around?" she asked, ignoring his not-so-humble brag. "I mean, there are so many magical creatures now. Where were you all before the end of the world?"

"Not the end of the *world*," he reminded her, "just human civilization. Oh, hmm, most of us were around. Hiding. That was an art we monsters had to master if we wanted to survive in the world you knew."

"So, all the sightings—creatures like the Loch Ness monster and Bigfoot—were they real?"

"I cannot attest to the validity of every instance, but sometimes, I'm sure, they were real."

Cher had millions more questions, but no chance to ask them; the fluttering of wings cut her off as a bird the size of an eagle landed on the kelpie's saddle horn.

It was a worn, old bird. Its graying, ratty feathers must once have been vivid shades of yellow, red, and orange— maybe even gold. Many of them looked gnawed. Its gray beak was scraped and scuffed, the tip chipped. It stared at Cher with one eye, then blinked slowly.

"Hello, Chum," it said to the kelpie telepathically. "Long time, no see. Looks like you got yourself a witch. How's the life of a familiar treating you?"

"What? Me?" The kelpie snorted. "No. I am not her *familiar*. We are...associates."

The bird narrowed its eyes. "Right."

The kelpie tightened his jaw and huffed out a sigh through his nostrils. He was *not* a familiar. Such a title might be worthy of a cat or a toad or a raven—even a phoenix, like the one on his saddle horn—but not a kelpie. It was beneath him. Humans, including the magical kind like Charity, were food, not friends.

And yet...

I was worried I hurt you, that's all.

Those words had slipped away from him after he'd accidentally cut Charity. He'd told himself then it was a lie, that he only cared for her because he needed her in tiptop shape when they finally came face-to-face with the hunters.

But that was only part of it. There was something else.

The taste of her blood—it had repulsed him. It had tasted *wrong*. Why? He had never had such a reaction to a living human's taste before.

He turned his nose back towards her now and sniffed, suddenly noticing how sour she smelled to him.

Perhaps I'm catching a cold, he thought. *Or maybe I'm so attached to her now the thought of eating her...*

No. No. He shook his mane, and the phoenix let out an irritated chirp at the sudden movement. *I'm sure she'll taste fine once it's time to eat.*

"You're up late," he said to the bird, eager to change the subject. "Isn't it well past your bedtime?"

"I haven't burned in days. The old lady's been pacing nonstop." His words were blunt, but there was an edge of concern in the bird's tone. "What brings you to this neck of the woods?"

"Um, excuse me?" Charity interrupted, and the kelpie realized she had been unable to hear their conversation this whole time. "Do you, uh, want me to shoo this bird off your back? Is it—is it dangerous? Will it attack me?"

The crest of limp feathers on the bird's head shot up, and Cher flinched; but instead of lunging at her, it only preened itself.

"What does she think I am, a goose?" he said to the kelpie.

"He's an old friend," the kelpie said to Cher. "He can stay. Charity Olmstead, meet Sunny the phoenix. His kind are peaceful and polite creatures. No need to worry. And this one happens to be the familiar of the witch who is going to train you."

"Oh." She reached out a tentative hand. Sunny flattened his crest and ducked his head, granting her permission to pet him. "Nice to meet you, Sunny."

The phoenix cooed softly, spread his wings wide, and bowed.

"You know what a familiar is, don't you?" the kelpie asked Cher.

"Of course," she replied. "A witch's animal companion. They're supposed to give some sort of magical boost to the witch, right?"

"Not *'supposed'* to. They do."

"Right. Of course. Because magic's real after all." She paused, and the kelpie could practically hear the gears turning in her head. "My parents both had their own cats, and one of their friends had a raven. I didn't know phoenixes could be familiars though.... Can any creature be a familiar, or is it only certain kinds?"

"Hang on, you gonna answer my question?" Sunny asked the kelpie, who was relieved once more for a change in subject. "Whatcha doin' here so far away from your river? You finally here to pay a visit to little ol' me?"

"We're here to see your mistress, actually," said the kelpie. "Miss Olmstead needs some training of the magical sort, and from the stories you've told me, your witch is one of Salem's most powerful."

"Yeah. Huh." Sunny shifted his weight. "I'll fly ahead and let her know you're coming. Or I'll try, at least."

"What do you mean?"

"Never mind," Sunny said. "Just follow the—"

"—The wisps, yes, I know. I couldn't possibly forget."

"Well, I wouldn't't'a had to repeat myself so much if you just took the damned invitation the first time," Sunny said as he hopped up onto the kelpie's head. For good measure, he pecked at his ear. A tiny piece of it came off in his beak. "Shit, sorry. Man, you're rotten."

"Just go," the kelpie sighed. "We can catch up while Miss Olmstead studies."

"We'll see." Sunny kicked off the kelpie's head, the gust from his wings sending nearby will-o-the-wisps bobbing like buoys in the air.

"What does that mean? Why are you being so dodgy?" the kelpie called. No answer. He shook his head. "Damn that one."

He trotted in the same direction Sunny had disappeared, lost in thought. What a strange encounter. Sunny usually never kept his beak shut, but the kelpie couldn't shake the feeling the phoenix was holding something back this time.

Charity eventually broke the silence. "So, hey," she said, "does this mean you're my famili—?"

"Absolutely not."

"But—"

"Kelpies are not familiars."

She frowned. "Fine then," she muttered, and they rode on without another word to each other.

Chapter Seven

The will-o-the-wisps led them through the forest for what felt like both forever and not long enough. On the one hand, Cher was eager to meet her mentor; on the other, she didn't want their stroll to end. She took in everything with hungry eyes.

Some of the trees she recognized: a hawthorn—like the one that had sprouted outside of her apartment; several oaks and maples. But then there were others she'd never seen before, with pink, purple, and silver leaves, black and golden bark. Some mushrooms she saw were as small as her thumb, but others were as tall as trees. There were spider-webs she could lie in like hammocks, and burrows that could have been home to giant rabbits.

It wasn't all beautiful though. Sometimes the wisps' lights caught a human corpse, pierced by a tree root or hanging broken in the branches overhead. And, more than once, a growl cut through the beautiful bird- and insect-song, too close for comfort.

But the kelpie always growled back, and whatever

lurked just out of sight decided Charity wasn't worth the fight.

When the wisps suddenly vanished, the kelpie froze.

"This is not supposed to happen," he said. "Sunny said they're supposed to lead us to a wall of willow trees. Do you see any willows?"

Cher noticed the fear around the edges of his voice and her blood turned cold. "No," she said. Without the wisps it was too dark for her to see much of anything beyond the glow of the kelpie's esca.

He reached out with his mind's voice, probing for the phoenix. "Sunny?" he called into the dark.

All Cher could hear was the sound of her own pounding heart, so loud in her ears it drowned out the sounds of the forest's wildlife.

No, that wasn't right. There were simply no other sounds to hear. Everything—all the creatures, and even the gentle breeze—had stilled under the oppressive shadows.

Something was wrong.

The familiar, heavy weight of despair dropped down onto Cher's shoulders out of nowhere, seizing hold of her heart. She held a hand to her aching chest, the knuckles of her other hand white around the saddle horn. Utter depression returned with a vengeance, as if it begrudged her the joy she'd felt after one day with the kelpie.

More than ever before, she wanted death.

She stifled the sudden compulsion to drop off her companion's back and provoke him until he had no choice but to kill her. To climb a tree and throw herself from its highest branches.

Unaware of her struggle, the kelpie fought his own battle. The half-healed wound on his neck burned as he remembered the bite of the hunter's blade. He heard the dying screams of his mate echoing all around him, as if all the birds of the forest were mimicking her death throes. And the blood, the smell of her blood...

It was all so vivid. He couldn't take it.

Forgetting Charity, he took several uneven steps backwards as if he could escape the memories closing in all around him. His hindquarters bumped against a tree trunk, and like cornered prey, all hope left him. His knees buckled.

Jostled, Cher lost her grip on the saddle and fell to the ground where she rolled to the outer edges of the esca's glow.

The circle of light shrank, and not by the kelpie's doing. As if the darkness were alive, it crept up Cher's legs and lower torso. She rolled onto her back and looked up.

There, hovering above her, she could just make out a humanoid shape floating in the shadows. It had scraggly, dank hair and long fingernails reaching for her. Two milky-white eyes reflected what little light was left, then flashed ice-blue as she made eye contact.

Pain pierced her forehead. Images flashed across her vision: nooses, chains, tables full of frighteningly sharp devices. Someone she couldn't see pinned down her wrists, another her ankles. She kicked and screamed. She thought she heard someone else screaming in unison with her...a child's scream—

A sudden white light washed out everything, banishing the darkness and blinding her. The hands holding her down disappeared, the screaming faded, and—though fear remained—the pure instinct to survive returned to her.

She rolled over and pushed to her feet again as her eyes gradually adjusted to the light.

The kelpie lay under a tree behind her, his esca extinguished and his head hanging low. He breathed heavy, ragged breaths, and his lidless eyes were full of wild terror.

Cher rushed to his side, dropping to her knees and wrapping her arms around his neck, muttering soothing words to him. She had no idea what he'd gone through, whether he'd seen the same things she had or terrors of his own.

All she knew was she hated to see him so afraid.

He did not push her away, did not snap at her, but rather leaned against her, trembling violently.

Sunny landed on the ground in front of them, warily tilting his head at the sight of his monstrous friend so cowed.

"I'm sorry it took me so long," he said to the kelpie, his usual irreverence missing. "I came as fast as I could."

Upon noticing Sunny, it finally occurred to Cher to check their surroundings and discover the source of the new light. It came from a lantern dangling from a gnarled walking stick. The flame inside was small but mighty, its glow warm after the freezing grip of the dark. It was no ordinary flame, but a magical one, attended by three will-o-the-wisps fluttering around inside the lantern. As Cher watched, they danced a little faster around the ball of white fire and it grew brighter; when they slowed, the light dimmed again.

An old woman clutched the walking stick and smiled in the lantern's glow.

Cher guessed she must be the witch they'd come to see,

and, for a second, all the horror of the last few moments shrank away as a thrill crept up her spine.

This woman was to be her mentor. And what a grand, fairy tale-worthy entrance she'd made.

The many wrinkles of her face were caked with dirt, like stripes; leaves and twigs stuck in her two long, white braids. She wore several layers of brown and gray robes, and dozens of crystal rings, necklaces, and bracelets that clinked together with her slightest movement. Her walking stick was a simple oak branch with no intricate carvings, but it was taller than she was. She had hammered a rusting nail into its knotty top, and it was from that nail the lantern swung.

When the old woman saw the kelpie, she showed no fear. Instead, she joined Cher beside him, bending at the waist to pat him between the ears. He gave a halfhearted growl, but she and Cher both hushed and calmed him.

"We must go quickly," said the old witch. Sunny alighted on her shoulder. "It isn't safe to linger out here for too long. Follow me."

She stood up straight and waited patiently for the kelpie to climb unsteadily back up onto his hooves.

"Let's go," Cher said to him, smiling even as she felt a tear drip off the tip of her nose. She hated seeing him like this. "Up-up."

"Stop stealing my line," he said, returning to his old self a bit.

Nevertheless, he stuck close to Cher as they followed the witch and her familiar for another twenty minutes or so.

Eventually, they came to the wall of willows they'd expected to find sooner. The trees grew so closely together,

Cher was sure it was impossible to pass through; their thick trunks and tangled branches truly did form a wall, like the bramble hedge around Sleeping Beauty's castle. Perhaps even denser than that, though not quite so sharp. Surely, it was a dead end. If anyone tried to get through the willow-wall, they would just end up trapped like a fish in a net.

"This is Fort Lee," the old woman said. "Or it used to be. As you can see, Willows Park has sort of...invaded it."

She reached up for one of the sweeping branches and gave it a gentle tug. The trees parted like curtains, forming a lavish, earthy archway, and revealing stone stairs embedded in the dirt. Relics of the former Fort Lee, Cher guessed.

The will-o'-the-wisps bobbed ahead of them to the other end of the path, where moonlight shone down into a clearing.

Their guide crooked a finger, beckoning them to follow. When they passed under the last of the arching branches, they stepped into a living fairy tale.

The stairs must have been all that was left of the fort, for the rest was wild.

In the center of the clearing was an ancient rowan tree, flourishing, with the brightest red berries Cher had ever seen. Dozens of birds of all colors perched within its branches, ruffling their feathers, chirping and chattering at one another.

"Is that—a *troll?*" Cher whispered incredulously, and the old woman smiled and nodded.

The troll in question sat beneath the rowan tree, a tiny book lying open in one of her huge palms. She was nearly three times the size of an average human, with stone-gray skin, giant fangs, and great ram-horns curling out of her temples.

As the archway fell shut at Cher's back, the troll barely spared them a glance, too absorbed in her book.

At the troll's feet was a shining pond, the starlight twinkling on its surface; and there, with his arms in the grass and his chin resting on his folded, webbed hands was what Cher could only assume was a naiad. The skin of his face was blue-green, his eyes round and golden like a frog's, and his iridescent fish's tail splashed up and down lazily behind his head. He waved to the kelpie, his fellow aquatic creature, and the kelpie gave a friendly nod in return.

"This way, please," the witch said, snapping Cher out of her daze.

She led them to the other end of the glade, where a cliff of solid, hard-packed dirt loomed. Trees lined the top of it, and in its wall was a cave. Roots hung down over the mouth to offer some privacy.

Outside of the cave was a fire pit with an authentic pewter cauldron hanging over it. Something—tea, maybe, or a strong herbal soup—already boiled within it, and a short creature that was little more than a leaf-bearded head with spindly arms and legs stirred the contents. A huge, horned beetle crawled through his beard, clicking its thick wings together and buzzing contentedly.

"Here we are," said the old woman.

Beside the fire was a table for two, with a decorative wine bottle that had been emptied of its original contents and instead filled with moss and leaves and twigs to create a centerpiece; tiny fireflies flashed all the colors of the rainbow inside the terrarium, adding one last enchanting touch to the clearing.

Sunny kicked off the old witch's shoulder and landed on a perch beside the table, a thick, L-shaped branch stuck in the ground. His dull tail feathers trailed in the dirt.

"Welcome to my humble abode," the old woman said, turning to face her guests and extending her arms. "My name is Evelyn Wyse. I hear you need help."

Chapter Eight

C harity waited for the kelpie to take the lead and explain to Ms. Evelyn Wyse exactly why they needed help. But instead he pushed her forward with his nose.

"Go on," he said. "I cannot talk to her. This is up to you."

When Cher glanced at him questioningly, he explained, "You see all those crystals she's wearing? My magic is useless against her. That includes telepathy." His brow knitted with worry. "That means she can't communicate with Sunny either. Strange..." He sniffed, shook his head. "Perhaps she just needed a break from him. He is an obnoxious chatterbox after all."

Cher shot him a glare: *Be nice.*

"Um," she said, clearing her throat and turning to their hostess. "H-hi, Evelyn. It's nice to meet you. Thank you so much for saving us back there. My name's Charity Olmstead, and—"

"Olmstead?" Evelyn's thin, white eyebrows shot

halfway up her forehead. "I know you. You're Roslyn and Theodore's little girl."

"Oh," said Cher, her voice straining with surprise. "Yes! You knew them? What am I saying? Of course you did." Everyone in Salem had known the Olmsteads.

"Not just them. I knew *you* too. Last time I saw you, you were a tiny, curly-haired lump swaddled in a blanket. Everyone said one day you'd become one of the most powerful witches in Salem, given your parents' abilities."

Her eyes narrowed. She touched an index finger to her lips thoughtfully, then said, "You know, I offered to be your godmother when you came of age. But word on the street was you turned down the offer to learn the craft on your thirteenth birthday."

"I—yes," Cher admitted. There was no use denying it. That was the main reason she was here, after all. Still, something in Evelyn's presence made her feel like she was a student in trouble with the principal, and she shifted her weight from one foot to the other. "It's just...the craft seemed to me a lot like religion, and I wasn't feeling partic ularly...um...faithful, by the time I was a teenager. Does that make sense? It all just seemed, I don't know...like empty promises, I guess?"

"You don't have to explain it to me," said Evelyn, shrugging.

"Right." Cher squared her shoulders and exhaled. "Well, it doesn't matter what choice I made," she said, "because, since the world ended, I see the dead. There's no escaping my heritage anymore, not with the way things are now."

Evelyn's expression brightened with curiosity.

"You don't say," the old witch muttered. "Well, Charity,

why don't you stay for a chat? Help yourself to a little soup and water. It will be refreshing after the fright you just had."

The leaf-bearded creature beside the cauldron stepped aside and offered Cher the ladle he'd been using. Meanwhile, the creature in the pond dove underneath the surface and returned with a sparkling glass of water—purified, perhaps, by magic.

Only then did Cher realize how hungry and thirsty she was. She'd gone over forty-eight hours without any food or water, many of those spent trekking through the wilderness, and suddenly she felt as though she might collapse. How she hadn't yet was beyond her. Something about being with the kelpie had distracted her from her dry throat and hollow stomach.

Once she settled into a seat with a steaming wooden bowl of what smelled like chicken broth with carrots and celery, the kelpie left the witches to talk. He joined the naiad in the pond for a swim.

"What was that thing that attacked us?" Cher asked. She took one sip of the water, paused, then immediately guzzled the rest. Little leaf-beard took her cup and dashed back with a refill. By the time he returned, she'd already finished off her soup as well, ignoring the way it burned her tongue.

Evelyn shuddered visibly. "That was what I've named the Devourer. Every psychic's worst nightmare," she said. "It is an evil magic..." Sipping a spoonful of her own soup, she gave Cher a glance up-and-down. "I see no crystals, so I take it you see the dead plain as the living?"

Cher nodded.

"The Devourer is one of the dead, corrupted by the

darkest magic," Evelyn explained. "The worst magic. An ancient and powerful spell, spoken with the cruelest intent and bound to an unlucky soul. I have a hunch I know where this one came from, but I cannot be sure."

"What do you know?" Cher asked. "Anything you can tell me is helpful. I don't understand anything about ghosts."

Evelyn set her bowl down and leaned forward in her chair, elbows resting on the table. "The dead cannot come into this clearing," she said. "I've placed crystals all around the perimeter. But I still see them lurking. When you look at a ghost, you can guess how long it's been dead. If they have a blue or white tint, they're still relatively fresh. If they're dull and gray, they're older. Much older. And there *are* a few old ghosts, very old ghosts, sniffing around Salem since the world ended. Ghosts I thought had been banished long ago."

She paused, took another sip of soup.

Then she named them: "Samuel and Betty Parris. Abigail Williams. Cotton Mather."

There wasn't a witch in Salem who didn't know those names. Even the kelpie, listening from the pond, felt a chill pass down his spine.

"The accusers," Cher said. "From the Witch Trials, right?"

It was Betty Parris and Abigail Williams, two little girls, who threw the first accusations. Betty's father, Samuel—and his fellow minister, Cotton Mather—were two of the most notorious leaders of the trials, organizing the court that sentenced twenty-five alleged witches to death by hanging.

Evelyn gave an affirmative hum.

"I've seen none of the accused, oddly enough," she said. "At least not yet. Which is a pity, because I think they would help stop whatever their accusers are up to this time around. They deserve their rest though, I suppose." She shook her head.

"The Devourer showed me visions." Cher suddenly lost her appetite, holding her half-finished soup in her lap. "Nooses. Torture devices. I think...maybe it was a threat? Maybe it's trying to repeat history?"

"It could be," said Evelyn. "I've suspected for a while now whoever created the Devourer used one of the souls of the accusers. Doing so would give an already evil spell an extra boost."

She set her bowl in her lap, rested her chin on her hand, and with the other she reached out and stroked the phoenix's head. "Sunny here recently went out for a morning flight, and when he returned, he had news." She took a slow breath. "Something...*concerning*...is happening over in Danvers."

The little food in Cher's stomach churned. It was a common misconception that the Witch Trials of 1692 started in what was now the city of Salem. It was actually the next town over, Danvers—formerly called Salem Village—where the first fateful accusation was made. That was where the Parris family had lived.

"Dozens of survivors have built two walled-in communities there," Evelyn explained. "One for surviving, and a smaller one for training soldiers...and holding trials. There's a gallows in the center of the second one." Her expression turned grim. "I suppose it isn't all that surprising. If history does repeat itself, it would start there."

"But why?" Cher asked, breathless. "Why would they do that?"

"Isn't it obvious? They believe witches caused the apocalypse—and now they're hunting us in retribution."

Bile rose in Cher's throat.

The kelpie's voice slipped into her mind. "What if these witch hunters are the same ones who killed my mate?" Then, he asked Sunny, "Did you see any of the accusers' ghosts in Danvers?"

"No," Sunny answered. "But if they haven't already, I'm sure they'll stick their fingers in that business soon enough."

Despite the warm soup in her belly, Cher's blood chilled in her veins and goosebumps crawled up her arms. Whatever trouble was brewing, there would be no avoiding it.

Not for a witch like her.

"Can you teach me to protect myself from the ghosts, at least?" she asked Evelyn.

"This should help a little." The old woman took off one of her many necklaces and passed it to Cher. "Psychic protection."

Before the kelpie could tell her not to, Charity put the necklace on.

Dammit.

It was one of the amethysts; not only did it protect Charity from ghosts, but it protected her from any psychic interference at all—including his.

The stupid old woman had just blocked his only line of communication with his companion.

A strange expression crossed Evelyn's face, and she glanced in his direction. He set one hoof on dry land, about to haul himself up out of the pond to try and tell Charity through gestures to take the necklace off again, when something snagged his back leg.

He kicked, but he could not shake off whatever it was.

A whiff of cunning drifted from Evelyn's direction, though it was hard to detect her intentions under the energy of all those crystals.

Whatever the case, the kelpie didn't like where this was going. He was about to shriek out a warning when whatever had him by the ankle dragged him under the water.

"I have something else," Evelyn said to Cher, who was oblivious to everything going on behind her. The old witch climbed to her feet with the help of her walking stick. "Follow me."

Cher followed her to the mouth of the cave. Evelyn stood just inside, the shadows obscuring all but her chin and her lips, which had spread into a strange smile.

Cher hesitated.

The kelpie strained against his bindings and kicked free long enough to break the pond's surface. He screamed so loud his throat ached.

Startled, Cher whipped around to see what was the matter—and felt something strike the back of her head.

Chapter Nine

She awoke in a dimly lit room with dirt-and-stone walls and roots dangling from the ceiling.

Beneath her was a mattress. The bed frame was made of thick, twisting tree branches that looked as though they had been grown and shaped by magic. Her wrists and ankles were tied around those branches with dry, chafing rope. The back of her head throbbed.

She thrashed against her bonds, but that only made her head hurt worse. Trying to calm her breath, she grew still and looked around the room instead.

Evelyn's walking stick was propped against the wall beside the bed, the lantern providing little light as the will-o-the-wisps rested at the bottom of their glass cage. Beside that was a birdbath full of...not water, but ashes and charred, blackened feathers. Sunny was nowhere to be seen. Another table like the one outside stood in the room's center, a book with yellowing pages open atop it.

Evelyn hunched over the tome, her hands shaking as

she read through the text with a pointed finger and muttered under her breath: "Yes, yes...no...perfect!"

Cher hadn't quite registered the amount of danger she was truly in until Evelyn looked up from the book and grinned a gray-toothed smile through the dark.

This was not the wise and quirky witch of the woods, the fairy godmother Cher had hoped for; Evelyn was deranged and *hungry* by the look in her eyes—more like the witch of Hansel and Gretel fame. Her braids had come undone completely, the ribbons untied and tangled in the ends of her messy hair. Her cheeks were flushed and sweat beaded her brow and upper lip as she picked up a mortar and pestle and ground something inside of it. She gnashed her teeth and kept her eyes on Cher the whole time, unblinking, just like the kelpie.

The kelpie.

"*Help!*" Cher screamed for him, pulling and kicking against the ropes.

Where was he? Why couldn't she hear him? Why had he led her here, to this wicked witch's lair?

"Oh, Charity," Evelyn tutted. "There's no need to scream. Anyway, your friend is a bit...preoccupied."

She approached the bed with the mortar in one hand and a vicious knife in the other.

"What do you want with me?" Cher said, unable to keep a sob from her voice. She wanted more than ever to die...but not like this. Not like this.

Evelyn tucked the knife into a pocket of her robes and dipped her thumb into the bowl.

"You see," she said, smearing a sour-smelling paste across Cher's forehead, down her nose, and dabbing it on her cheeks, "I cannot be your mentor. When the world ended, I lost my magic. *Poof!* It just disappeared. And what use would I be to you without it?"

The old woman's eyes flashed with anger. "Do you know how maddening it is?" she said. "To see the dead, but not be able to speak with them anymore? To live in a world overflowing with magic, and have none of it for yourself?

"I've been trying to get my powers back for weeks now," she continued, smearing the paste in strange patterns on her own face. "Then along you come, just bursting with magical energy. The Olmsteads' little girl. Who would have thought?

"I have tried everything; every trick in my grimoire even mundane folks could do. Prayers, meditation, potions, animal sacrifice. Nothing has brought my magic back. But there is one last ritual I can try now that you're here."

She paused. Her grin stretched wider and wider yet.

"An exchange of blood between two witches."

Evelyn turned and set the mortar down on the table, returning with the knife.

"Let's be honest, Charity," she said. "I'm better-equipped than you are to deal with the future looming over Salem. Wiser and more experienced. Why should I waste time teaching you everything I know when I could just take the burden of your powers away from you and do everything myself?"

She pricked her own thumb with the knife.

"Besides, you don't really *want* to be a witch, do you?" She clicked her tongue. "Such a scandal it was, the Olmsteads' own daughter turning her back on them like that all those years ago. Talk of the town. Not that *I* judged you. Being a witch comes with great responsibility. Not everyone wants that." She watched the blood well up and drip down her knuckles. "Think of it this way: I'm doing you a favor, Charity. You never asked for these powers, did you, sweetheart? Let me help you. Let me take them."

The reflection of her teeth glinted in the knife's polished blade.

"Open wide."

Without waiting for Cher to obey, Evelyn jabbed her thumb between her victim's lips so forcefully her nail cut Cher's mouth. She choked as the witch's blood pooled on her tongue.

"Now, I'm afraid," Evelyn said as she pressed Cher's jaw shut with her free hand, "that my grimoire only contains directions for a ritual to borrow a teeny-tiny boost of magic from another witch. I believe, to transfer the full extent of your powers to me, I will need much more of *your* blood than you need of mine. I'm so sorry, Charity."

She withdrew a goblet from the folds of her robe.

"I promise to make this little experiment as painless as possible."

Back in the clearing, the kelpie was indeed preoccupied. The troll had dragged him out of the little pond, after the naiad bound him with thick seaweed and prevented him from chasing after Evelyn and Charity; now the troll held him like a toy in one of her giant hands, fingers wrapped around his middle lifting him a dozen feet off the ground. Kick and shriek and snap as he might, the troll remained unperturbed, holding her tiny book open in her other hand and reading on as if the kelpie didn't exist at all.

Sunny landed in the branches of the rowan tree above the troll's head.

"Why are you so mad?" the phoenix asked, cocking his head to one side as he watched the kelpie's futile struggle.

"What is that old hag doing to her?" the kelpie snarled.

"Relax. She's just performing a blood ritual."

The kelpie's eyes looked like they might pop out of their sockets. "*A blood ritual?*"

"Yep. She needs Charity's magic, y'see. Lost her own after the world ended. I've been trying to help her get it back, but we've had no luck."

"*Charity* needs Charity's magic," the kelpie said. "*I* need Charity's magic."

Sunny twisted his head the other way. "What's wrong? You worried if she ain't a witch anymore, she won't need a familiar? Don't worry about that. Evelyn's got no powers and I'm still—"

"I am *not* Charity's familiar," the kelpie snarled. "None of that matters to me. My mate is dead, Sunny. Whatever those bloody ghosts of Salem's past are up to, they had something to do with her slaughter. If I'm going to get revenge, then I need Charity Olmstead's help."

"Aw, I'm sorry to hear about your mate," Sunny said, not insincerely. Still, there was a level of nonchalance in the way he preened his feathers that irritated the kelpie. "But if all you need's a psychic, then why not just let Evelyn take Charity's powers? She plans on stopping whatever those ghosts are up to anyway. I'm sure she'd help you get your revenge if I explained the situation to her."

The kelpie gritted his teeth. "It needs to be Charity."

"And why's that? Why can't it just be any old psychic?"

"Charity and I already made a deal," the kelpie said,

though he knew it was a weak explanation. "A blood contract. And I have far too much dignity to break my promise to her."

Sunny hopped down to an even lower branch of the tree, clacking his beak teasingly. "You can still uphold your end of the bargain if you let Evelyn take over, can't you? Unless what you promised her has something to do with her learning how to control her magic. Then I can understand why you're insistent on stopping Evelyn."

The kelpie did not answer him.

"I take your silence as a 'no.'" Sunny paused, waited for the kelpie to correct him. He didn't. "That settles it. Nothing's stopping you from keeping your promise and Evelyn's little ritual should be no problem for you."

"I—"

Charity's voice drifted out from the cave, floating up into the night sky, "*Help!*"

The kelpie kicked his legs again, though they met nothing but open air. The troll paid him no mind.

"Put me down!" the kelpie growled at her. "Sunny, tell her to let me go."

The phoenix continued fussing with his feathers. "Sorry, pal," he said, "but Evelyn's been driving me nuts. She's always got me out looking for this or that potion ingredient or ritual material, and the few chances I *do* get to rest my wings, she's keeping me up with all her mumblin' and pacing. Whenever I tell her to get some rest herself, she blocks me out with those stupid crystals. I told you, I ain't burned in ages. I need Evelyn to take Cher's magic as much as she does. Maybe then she'll shut up for a while and we can both get some sleep."

"You bastard." The kelpie nearly strained his back, he

thrashed so hard against the troll's grip, snapping his jaws in the phoenix's direction. "I'll kill you!"

Sunny narrowed his beady little eyes. "Now that isn't a very nice thing to say to your friend. Look, I get it. I know what it's like to be a witch's familiar. To love 'em so much you'd do anything to protect 'em. Just admit you care about her—"

Another scream came from inside the nearby cave, so piercing even the troll looked up from her book, and Sunny flapped his wings, startled.

The kelpie went limp. "*Please,* Sunny."

Desperation crept into his voice. Desperation and shame. This was no way for a kelpie to act, begging on a human's behalf. So much for dignity.

"Wait here." There was an edge of panic in Sunny's voice. "Something's not..." He didn't finish explaining. Instead, he launched himself from the rowan tree and disappeared into the cave's shadowy entrance.

An agonizingly long moment passed before he returned.

"Be a doll and let him go," the phoenix said, gently poking his beak at the troll's knuckles. "This is bad. Real bad." The words were clipped with worry. "Be careful with him now," he told the troll. "'Atta girl." To the kelpie he said, "Come fetch your witch, please."

The kelpie needed no permission. Before Sunny even finished speaking, he'd already rushed into the cave, expecting the worst.

* * *

What had happened when Evelyn touched that hideous knife to Cher's throat—for it was the throat she'd aimed to cut, and not the palm or thigh or something far less deadly —was a lucky accident: the leather cord of the crystal necklace Evelyn had gifted to her ripped before Cher's neck did.

And in that split second before blade met skin, as Cher screamed bloody murder, a breeze tickled her cheek and a voice whispered in her ear a single word: *"Fire."*

Her blood burned warm in her veins and her palms ached. There were flames inside of her, and they wanted out, *out.*

As if someone had struck flint to steel, a spark caught the tip of Evelyn's wide sleeve. In her panic, the old woman dropped the knife, and—though it wasn't high enough above Cher's neck to cut very deep as it fell—it still sliced a thin, painful line before gravity knocked it down onto its flat side and left it discarded on her collarbone.

"No!" Evelyn screamed.

"Again," the voice said into Cher's ear, friendly and encouraging. *"Fire."*

She focused, then, on the ropes binding her wrists, ignoring the ruckus Evelyn was making as she tried to stifle the flames crawling up her arm. Just as before, Cher wanted fire and it appeared, willed into existence. Easy as pie.

No, easy as *magic.*

Her wrists were pink and tender from the flames, but she was free. She shook the last charred remains of the rope away, took up Evelyn's dropped knife, and cut the bindings off her ankles.

"Cher!"

The kelpie stood, chest heaving, in the archway of Evelyn's chamber. As he called out to her, he was unable to hide the relief in his voice.

She didn't greet him, though she was just as happy to see him unharmed. Shock had seized hold of her. Their visit—dreamlike from the moment they'd stepped into the glade—had taken a nightmarish turn. And, with the magic pumping through her veins, everything looked and sounded twice as strange. Both sharp and fuzzy at once. Unreal, despite her heightened senses.

Fear gave way to giddiness, and her steps across the chamber were light and shaky.

She didn't spare Evelyn so much as a glance, even as the old witch stopped batting at her sleeve, roared, and made a grab for Cher.

She missed.

Cher sidestepped, her hip bumping against the little table with the book open on top of it.

Without conscious thought, Cher pressed the book's cover closed, lifted it, and tucked it under her arm.

"Don't you dare—!" Evelyn began, but Cher still held the knife. She pointed it at the old woman until Evelyn backed off and stepped aside.

The kelpie turned to follow as Cher exited the chamber, brushing his shoulder against hers. They ran side-by-side through the tunnel and out of the cave, back into the clearing.

Evelyn's heavy, labored breath and the crackling of the fire slowly, oh so slowly, crawling up her sleeve sounded behind them.

"*Stop them!*" she screamed, as Cher swung herself up into the kelpie's saddle and they galloped past the fire-pit, the pond, the rowan tree and the troll beneath it, to the wall of willows.

The troll climbed slowly, laboriously to her feet, and the kelpie galloped harder.

The magical archway had closed behind them when they arrived, but Cher reached up and tugged one of the branches, as she'd seen Evelyn do, and the trees opened up again.

Evelyn's screams chased them out. *"She stole my grimoire!"*

Cher glanced back and pity stung her heart. "Enough," she whispered, and the fire burning up Evelyn's sleeve was extinguished as abruptly as it had started.

Evelyn didn't seem to notice, or maybe she didn't care. *"After them!"* she commanded, voice shaking with rage and fear and despair.

"Hold on," the kelpie said, and the trees blurred as he raced faster than he'd ever run in his life, away from that horrible place.

Chapter Ten

The willows crawled closed once Cher and the kelpie were through, but they could feel the troll's lumbering footsteps as it followed them, could hear Sunny's wings flapping somewhere above the treetops. The kelpie doused the light of his esca and veered off the will-o-the-wisps' path, into the utter darkness of the thickest part of the forest.

"The Devourer," Cher warned him, remembering the shadow that had attacked them just before Evelyn came to their rescue. How happy she'd been to see the old witch in that moment—appearing like a fairy godmother.

"Don't worry. I remember," the kelpie said. "Though I wish I could forget. We'll keep an eye out."

"Did the Devourer show you what it showed me, or—?"

"Hush now please. They're looking for us."

Right on cue, they heard the willows creaking open somewhere behind them to let the troll through.

The kelpie made a point to take a path the troll would have difficulty navigating, where the trees grew closest together. Luckily, he could see just fine in the dark. He stepped lightly over roots and around bushes, careful not to rustle too much.

"Ol' buddy, ol' pal," came Sunny's voice into his mind, "I know you're down there. Just tell little Cherbear to give the book back and no harm done, okeydoke? Evie's been workin' on that thing her whole life."

The kelpie considered it for a heartbeat—at the very least, to get the old witch off their back—before he realized Cher's brilliance in stealing the grimoire. If Evelyn wouldn't teach her magic, then she could teach herself.

And what better way to learn than from the pages of one of Salem's most powerful witches?

He did not answer Sunny, but kept sneaking through the forest. Past giant spiderwebs, herds of ten-eyed deer, a bear's den.

The dragon's nest.

The trees were uprooted and bent, stomped down like tall grass where the dragon lay every day, soaking up the sunlight; but now the moon shone down on an empty nest. There were no bones, the kelpie noted. Perhaps this particular dragon wasn't carnivorous after all.

Or perhaps it simply preferred not to eat where it slept.

The kelpie crept along the outskirts, careful not to step out from beneath the cover of the trees in case Sunny was still on their trail. He sensed that Cher longed to stop and investigate, heard her thoughts as she took mental notes and tucked them away in the back of her mind as if she would do something with them later. As if she planned to live long enough to find a notebook and jot all her observations down.

As if she didn't want to die after all.

He longed to say, *I told you so*. But not yet. Not until they were safe.

Veering away from the dragon's nest, the kelpie carried Cher back into the depths of the forest, picking his way over roots, up and down the sloping earth, and finally coming to a halt at a narrow stretch of river. Warning Cher to hold her breath and cling to him, he dipped them both beneath the surface, swam swiftly upstream, and carried her to the opposite shore.

"That should get them off our trail," he said, though he still walked at a brisk canter.

He slowed only when he noticed an apple tree and ordered Cher to pluck a few for herself. Her adrenaline was wearing off fast, and using magic had left her weak and exhausted. She needed food, or she might collapse.

"Want one?" she asked, reaching down to hold one beside his face.

He sniffed. "No, thank you," he said. "Yuck."

"What kind of horse are you?" Cher said, shining the apple on the hem of her nightgown and taking a bite. Maybe it was the fact it was grown in an enchanted forest, or maybe it was because Evelyn's soup hadn't been very filling; whatever the case, it was the most delicious apple she'd ever eaten in her life, so sweet and juicy she had to fight herself to savor it.

"Not a horse," the kelpie said. "More closely related to fish."

"Whatever."

When she finished off the apple, Cher tossed the core away for the worms to enjoy and pulled the grimoire from inside her leather jacket, where she'd zipped it up nice and secure. She read by the moonlight filtering through the branches.

The book fell open automatically to the ritual spell Evelyn had just attempted.

Charity shuddered and quickly flipped back to the first page, scanning the table of contents the old witch had so lovingly and carefully curated over the years. Potion recipes were mixed in with spells of all kinds, from hexes to healing, over 400 entries crammed into 313 hand-numbered pages. Several blank pages had been added into the back to make more room, causing the black-and-silver book's leather spine to crack a little under the strain.

For half a second, Cher allowed herself to feel a tiny bit of guilt for stealing the grimoire. She knew, after all, how maddening and terrifying it was to be a psychic living in a world crawling with the dead, but to have no control over her powers at all.

At least—for her—there was hope she could yet learn; but for Evelyn, it was far worse. She'd had a taste of that power and protection. She'd known it her whole life, and now it was taken from her. If she couldn't find a way to get her magic back, she would be at the new world's mercy forever. The crystals were some help warding off the spirits, but if she ever lost them...

Cher's gaze landed on an entry in the table of contents labeled "Dealing with the Dead."

"Anything worthwhile?" the kelpie asked, as she flipped to page 166.

She read to herself for a few moments before answering. "Amethysts are best for psychic protection, which explains why Evelyn gave me one. Shit. I should have grabbed that necklace before we left. It fell off in the fight."

"Yes, but they work a little *too* well. You see, that's why I couldn't speak with you back there."

"I think protecting myself from ghosts is slightly more important than being able to talk to you," she snapped.

The kelpie flattened his ears against his skull.

"Sorry," she sighed. "I'm still on edge, from—you know, almost getting killed. You're right. There's got to be another way to protect myself."

"*I'm* sorry, Cher," the kelpie said before she could continue reading. "If I'd have known what sort of state Evelyn was in, I wouldn't have led you into her trap. Sunny was acting strange from the very moment he found us in the forest. I should have known something was wrong."

Cher softened. "It's okay," she said. "We got what we went there for. Sort of. Let's just—forget about it and keep moving."

"You know we're going to have to go to Danvers?" the kelpie asked. "I have no doubt that everything happening there is somehow connected to my mate."

A pause. "Yeah," said Cher. "I figured."

"Will you be ready?"

Another pause, heavier this time. "I'll try. I made a promise to you. And anyway," she said, shifting in the saddle, "I don't want to let Salem's history repeat itself. It's...it's nice, having a cause to fight for. Something worth dying for, before I actually—y'know—*die*. So. Thank you. For the opportunity."

There was a brief, awkward silence. Then, she went on, "I'll be honest. I still kind of have a defeatist feeling about it. Like, shit, we endured ten years of fascism and now I find out even at the end of the world it's still around. Like some bad virus your body can't quite shake. But things are different now. There's magic, and anyone can have the power if they just learn to wield it. Even *I* can have power, and—"

"Cher?" The kelpie interrupted her babbling.

"Mm?"

"Do you still want to die?" he asked. "When all this is over?"

She didn't answer right away.

"Yeah," she said eventually, but he sensed the insincerity in her heart. She did not want to die. He knew he was right, even if she wouldn't admit it—yet.

"As you wish."

When she spoke again, there was a forced chipperness to her voice. "I've thought of a name for you, by the way."

"Oh? Who said I wanted one?"

"Ferry."

"Fairy? Like one of those little winged pests?"

Cher laughed. "No, *Ferry*. Like a boat. F-E-R-R-Y."

"A boat?"

"It's a sort of vessel that—"

"I *know* what a boat is. Frankly, they're just as pesky as fairies. Why is this the name you've settled on?"

"Well, first of all—as much as I would love for us to be Sonny and Cher—you can't be Sonny-with-an-O because we already know a Sunny-with-a-U and that would just get confusing."

"I detest pop music anyway. More of a sea shanty fan myself."

Cher blinked. "How do you even know what pop music is?"

"I hear everything my prey thinks, remember? Sometimes they have songs stuck in their heads."

Cher smiled and shook her head. "Of course. Anyway, secondly, you're like the ferry from Greek mythology the dead sail across the River Styx to their afterlives. Ferrying off souls is technically what you do, isn't it? A little less peacefully, but you grant the final wishes of your prey. Even if you do, um—brutally tear them limb-from-limb."

"Sure, but why name me after an object and not the man who sails the boat?" He knew his Greek myths as well as the next monster. In fact, he considered Scylla a good friend of his. "Charon sounds much nobler than *Ferry*."

"Maybe. But your victims ride on your back the same way they ride the boat." She tugged playfully at a stringy clump of his mane. "Plus Ferry's funnier, because you hate it and you're fun to annoy."

The kelpie knew any other of his kind would protest and remind Cher he was a mighty monster, to be feared and respected. They were not friends. There was no affection between them.

But he was too tired to care just then. Or, at least, that was what he told himself. They'd been through hell, and so instead he sighed.

"Fine."

"You approve?" Cher couldn't keep the glee out of her voice.

"I don't approve, no. But I can tell you've made up your mind. So, Ferry it is."

"Nice!" She pumped a fist into the air. "Ferry it is."

* * *

The kelpie now known as Ferry watched the skies, but there was no sign of Evelyn's familiar anywhere. Nor could he hear the troll's rumbling footsteps, or feel them rattling the ground beneath his hooves. Hopefully, their pursuers had given up and returned to the glade to help Evelyn calm down.

Near dawn, Ferry and Cher finally reached the outskirts of the forest and arrived near Salem's north-eastern coast. He decided they were safe enough for now to step out from beneath the trees' cover.

The second they were out in open air, a heavy wind picked up. Panicking, Ferry backtracked to get under the canopy of leaves and branches—just as the dragon, queen of the forest, flew over their heads on her way back to her nest.

In that same moment, the waves in the Atlantic Ocean surged, crashing against the shore where once docks and seaside restaurants had stood. The rays of the rising sun caught something scaly breaking the surface of the water.

Another dragon. This one's scales were iridescent, reflecting the sky the same way the glittering sea did. It had a long, snake-like body and whiskers that dripped water as the creature lifted its enormous head to bask in the sunrise.

Ferry and Cher waited, enjoying the view—until the peace was shattered by a sudden splash and a crunch. When the sea-dragon lifted its head back above water, a thresher shark's long tail dangled between its teeth.

"Remind me not to swim in these waters anytime soon," Ferry said. "I'll stick to my river for now, thank you very much."

"Yeah, honestly, I'm having second thoughts about swimming with the whales," said Cher.

Appetite satiated for now, the sea-dragon slithered towards shore and carried itself up onto the sand with its short legs, curling up contentedly to watch the rest of the sunrise. It must be at least thirty feet long, Cher noted, and the gills peeking out from beneath its neck frills sealed themselves up while it was on dry land, just like the kelpie's did.

Ferry turned north, intending to stick close to the line of trees until they were well away from the sea-dragon. North was the Crane River, which they would eventually cross into Danvers.

"Wait," Cher whispered. She'd spotted something to the south that sent her pulse racing. "Turn around. Please."

"Danvers is *this* way," Ferry said, tossing his head insistently.

"Please?"

She would slip from the saddle and run south herself if he wouldn't take her. With a resigned huff, the kelpie turned them the way she wanted to go.

"What is it?" he asked.

"Look." Cher pointed.

Tangled in the gnarled roots of an oak tree was an old neon sign that read: *ARCADE*.

Ferry sensed several memories rushing through Cher's mind: afternoons racing home from school to get homework done and bike to the arcade with her friends; begging her parents for their spare quarters so she could play the claw machine over and over in the hopes of snagging the biggest stuffed animal before anyone else did; feeling on top of the world when she and her best friend topped the scoreboards on one of the zombie games; pushing their bikes home at sunset, their pockets stuffed full of tickets they were saving up for the top behind-the-counter prizes.

"You spent your early life in this neighborhood?" Ferry said.

"Yeah." There was a yearning in her tone. "Do you mind if we see whether my parents' house is still standing? I mean—I could use a rest. In a real bed."

She tempered herself, and Ferry sensed she was trying not to get her hopes up.

"They sold the house eight years ago, to a friend," she explained. "But...well, they put a spell on my apartment. Some sort of blessing. I think that's why it withstood the apocalypse. I bet you anything they did the same thing for the house. I know they haven't lived there for a while—but what if that blessing held up?"

"Sure," Ferry said. He was eager to get to Danvers, but if he didn't oblige, he knew Cher would be a pain.

Anyway, he was going to eat her eventually; the least he could do was grant her this one simple wish.

"We'll make it quick," he said, snappish and irritated—more with himself than with Cher.

The apocalypse had not been kind to the neighborhood Cher grew up in.

Though the dragon-fire hadn't touched it, the ocean had flooded its streets. Instead of being burned, many of the houses were nothing more than salt-stained wreckage strewn everywhere. There were still some bits of paved road left, though there were great cracks and gouges in the asphalt, and the grass on the lawns had grown unusually tall and wild in only two months.

As Ferry followed what was left of the street, Cher

dropped out of the saddle and walked beside him with a hand gently resting against his flank.

If she closed her eyes, she could imagine looking down at her old pink-and-green sneakers scuffing the sidewalk. She could remember the laughs of her friends.

The Coven Kids, they had called themselves. Raised by witches. God, she could hear those laughs so clearly she almost thought—

She snapped her eyes open as they rounded the corner.

There was home. The apocalypse-tossed sea had chipped and battered the house's paint, but the earth beneath its foundation had grown itself into a hill, protecting it from the worst of the storm; and so, it was still blessedly, miraculously, magically standing.

And sitting on the porch swing—Cher couldn't believe it.

"Maya," she breathed.

There were two Black women swinging together. One wore a septum ring and had her hair tucked neatly under a colorful wrap. Cher didn't recognize her.

But the other woman, resting her head on the stranger's shoulder, was unmistakably Maya Ambrose.

That laugh, carried on the soft breeze, was the same rich, witchy cackle Maya had perfected in high school. Her tattoos had multiplied since Cher last saw her; now her neck and legs were covered in ink, as well as her arms.

Cher's stomach twisted. She didn't know how to feel, seeing Maya sitting there on the porch of her childhood home, just like the old days.

Ferry tilted his head curiously.

"My ex-girlfriend," she explained as she tugged him towards a pile of wreckage they could hide behind. She had a feeling Maya wouldn't take kindly to an ex showing up on her block with a hideous monster in tow. "Maya and I grew up together and ended up dating for a few years in college."

She smirked to herself, shaking her head in disbelief as she glanced back up at the porch and watched Maya intertwine fingers with the other woman.

Exactly how many of her exes had survived the apocalypse? Would she run into more of them, or were Dean and Maya the only two she had to worry about?

The kelpie sniffed. "I sense things didn't end well between you two? Or else we wouldn't be hiding right now."

"Things didn't really *start* well with us."

Ferry didn't ask her to elaborate. He could just sift through her memories if he wanted to know badly enough.

Though she did hate that habit of his, she'd rather he just do that this once, instead of asking her to relive the whole story. She'd had years to reflect on their breakup now, and the whole thing was childish and embarrassing.

"Well, why don't you go say hello?" Ferry said after a while. "Maybe she can help."

"Help?"

"Maya is a witch, is she not?" the kelpie said.

Cher nodded. Maya was one of the original Coven Kids, and—unlike Cher—she chose to follow in her mother's footsteps when she turned thirteen.

"Perhaps she could help you make sense of some of the spells in Evelyn's grimoire," said Ferry. A logical conclusion to draw.

Cher hesitated.

"What is it? You think she hasn't forgiven you?" he asked. "Seven years is a long time."

"It isn't *that* long," she said quietly, shoulders slumped. "We said some...ugly things to each other, the day we broke up."

She wasn't sure she'd forgiven Maya yet; she wouldn't be surprised if Maya still held a grudge too.

Ferry sighed. "Well, maybe talking to her will make you both feel better then," he said. "Go talk to her. I'll wait here. And if she turns you away, I'll make sure she sees reason."

Cher laughed, but her smile was sad. She patted his cheek. "Thanks, you big softy," she said. "For encouraging me. It means a lot to me."

He *tsked*. "You humans are so sensitive." His tone was irritated, but Cher thought she heard a friendly, almost affectionate undercurrent.

"Says the kelpie who doesn't want to admit he's my familiar," she joked.

The mood between them shifted so fast, she barely had time to grasp what was happening.

Ferry suddenly snarled and snapped his jaws at her, making a horrible growling sound deep in his throat that scared off a nearby seabird.

She gasped and fell backwards into the damp grass, hands sinking into the mud. Whether he would really kill her or not, she didn't want to find out. She threw her hands up over her face and winced, prepared at the very least to lose some blood.

But no blow came, no teeth scraped against her forearms. She felt the kelpie's breath hot against her skin.

When she lowered her arms again, Ferry's huge and

hideous face was inches from her own, his lidless eyes spinning furiously in their sockets.

"Ferry, what the *hell*—?"

"Do not," he said, "forget what I am. And do not dare call me that foul word. *Familiar.*" He practically gagged.

Cher gritted her teeth, determined not to let him see she was frightened.

"Oh yeah?" she said. "Then why do you care about me at all? What does it matter to you if I fix things with Maya?"

Why he hated the thought of being her familiar so much, she didn't understand. Was it their contract? Did he feel guilty he had vowed to kill her at the end of all this? Or was it something else?

Whatever the case, it didn't matter. She *knew* she was right. She was sure he was her familiar, whether he liked it or not.

Surely he felt the magic flowing between them too? Surely he felt the same cold emptiness as she did when they'd been separated at Evelyn's glade, and surely his blood sparked with electricity when they were reunited, just like hers did.

Surely—the thought struck her—surely it was *Ferry's* voice that had called out to her, urging her to summon the flames that freed her. His soul calling out to hers, though perhaps neither of them even realized it. That was what a familiar was for, after all, to coax the magic out of a witch's heart.

"It *doesn't* matter to me," he said. "I don't give a toad's tongue if you repair your relationship or not." He took a sinister half-step towards her, his head and shoulders hunched low like a hound about to pounce. She backed up another few inches, but still defiantly held his gaze. "All that matters to me is that you are in fighting shape before we inevitably face the hunters. A means to an end—that is all you are to me, Charity Olmstead. We are not friends. I am *not your familiar.*"

He turned his back on her and stomped back the way they came.

"Where are you going?" she called after him.

"Away for a while," he said.

"But—"

"Go talk to your friend."

"Ferry!"

"I'll be back just before sunrise. We still have an oath to fulfill."

Chapter Eleven

C her jumped to her feet and almost chased after Ferry, but in the end she resisted. *Let him pout,* she decided. Eventually he'd see she was right. She could feel her magic ebbing the further he walked away from her. His absence already left her hollow. He'd come running back to her any second...

"Excuse me?"

A voice echoed down the block and Cher turned to see Maya and her friend—girlfriend, maybe?—standing at the bottom of the porch steps.

Staring straight at her.

"Shit," she muttered under her breath. Her argument with Ferry must have attracted their attention.

No choice now. She'd have to talk to them whether she was ready or not.

She raised both arms into the air, showing them she was a peaceful newcomer and not some bandit out to rob them. She could tell by the way Maya stood slightly in front of her partner, like a shield, they were wary of a stranger in the neighborhood.

Well—not a total stranger, but they didn't realize that yet.

Slowly, Cher waded up the flooded block to her old home.

"Hi," she called, and saw recognition flit across Maya's face. "Um. Hey. It's...it's me."

It was all she could think of to say. She was too dazed by it all—her old house so untouched at the top of the hill, the morning sun rising behind it like a halo, and Maya standing in the exact spot she used to wait whenever she dropped by for a visit.

Maya's partner glanced uncertainly between them. "You know this person?" she asked.

Maya crossed her arms. "Yeah," she said. "She's my ex." Her partner raised her eyebrows, but before she could ask any more questions, Maya raised her voice and said, "Hey, Charity. What brings you here?"

Cher saw right through the sweet tone. Maya wasn't happy to see her at all, her loathing seething through her forced smile.

Pasting an equally false smile on her face, Cher decided to play along. "I thought I'd swing by and see if my old home was still standing," she said, shifting her gaze to the house. "Looks like it is. Mind if I come in?"

Maya's smile dropped and her partner muttered something into her ear.

"Nothing to indicate she's got any bad intentions," Maya said, not bothering to whisper back.

"You don't think she's manipulating her own aura?" the other woman asked.

Ah. Cher understood then. Every witch had a specialty, and Maya's was reading auras. She must be checking now to make sure Cher didn't have any tricks up her sleeves.

Maya made a face like she smelled rotten fish. "She can't. Charity isn't a witch."

"You're wrong, actually," Cher replied, her false smile turning into a genuine one—a little smug, especially when she saw how Maya's face dropped. "I *am* a witch, now. Just not a very good one yet, if I'm honest." Seeing her chance to offer an olive branch, she asked, "Maybe you could help me out? At the very least, I could use somewhere to rest. Just for a day."

Maya's partner stepped forward. "Who were you arguing with earlier?" she asked. "We heard yelling."

"My familiar." Cher saw no point in lying. "We, um... aren't getting along right now."

"You have a familiar?" Maya sounded impressed. "What is it, a rat?"

"No." She ignored the veiled insult. "A...horse. Sort of."

"Sort of?"

"Yeah. Sort of." She didn't explain any further.

"And where did this sort-of-horse disappear to?" Maya asked.

"He threw a temper tantrum and went to walk it off." She shifted her weight from one bare foot to the other. "Look—I could really use some water and a comfortable chair. I've been riding in a saddle for ages. Can we talk inside?"

Maya's eyes narrowed and she sucked the inside of her cheek. "Interesting," she said. "Very interesting." There was a long pause while she surveyed the neighborhood from her high perch, no doubt double-checking Cher wasn't about to signal for backup and stage an ambush.

Once satisfied the coast was clear, she said, "Fine. You can come in."

* * *

Cher hesitated at the base of the hill. The lawn was as untamed as ever. Her parents had always allowed dandelions to flourish alongside their old garden, much to the neighbors' chagrin, only occasionally trimming the grass when it obscured their view out the windows. Their tiger lilies remained, a bright splash of orange against the white latticework of the porch. The winding path of steppingstones leading up the lawn remained as well.

Nothing changed, and everything changed.

Cher held her breath as the familiar creak of the porch steps sounded beneath her feet. Maya and her partner opened the front door and held it for her

When she finally crossed the threshold, it felt like stepping into a time machine.

Her parents had left behind much of their furniture for the friend who had bought the house. There was no need to lug it all with them to their fancy, fully-furnished retirement home down south. The couch had been replaced, but the new owner had simply reupholstered the old easychairs Teddy and Ros Olmstead used to sit in on either side of the fireplace.

It smelled the same too. Like sea breeze and cinnamon incense, though Cher didn't see any incense sticks around. She wouldn't be surprised if that scent had just permanently soaked into the house's foundation after her parents burned it almost every day.

A ginger Maine Coon waltzed into the living room from the bedroom hallway and froze at the sight of Cher. It was old and grungy, one ear torn as if it had been in a fight. A growl rose in its throat.

"Chill, Alistair," said Maya. "She's a friend."

Alistair hissed in response and darted back into the master bedroom.

"Little shit." Turning to Cher, Maya gestured to the narrow staircase on her right and said, "The attic's the same. Want to see it?"

"*Exactly* the same?"

"Exactly the same. Come on."

The three of them climbed the stairs single-file, and at the top Maya threw her shoulder into the door as she twisted the knob. That was always the trick to open it; the door was notoriously sticky, especially in warmer weather.

A half-wall divided the attic in two. On the right, smaller side of the room were some old boxes covered in layers of dust.

To the left—and also covered in dust—was Cher's old bedroom. A tiny twin bed with an off-white comforter and a floppy pillow lay underneath the porthole window overlooking the front lawn.

On the wall directly across from the door was a grand mural. Cher's parents made some extra money decorating the margins of witches' spellbooks. On their daughter's fifth birthday, when she officially moved into the "big-kid" attic bedroom, they'd used those artistic skills to paint her wall.

The mural depicted a witch in her garden. Bees and ladybugs buzzed happily around sunflowers and vegetables and fruit trees. The witch reached out a glowing, purple-nailed hand to pluck an apple from a branch, a blissful smile on her face. In the background was a forest, where a unicorn dashed between trees and fairies danced around a mushroom.

Cher stared at the mural, half thrilled it was still intact, and half guilty at the sight of it. She'd always hated looking at it after her thirteenth birthday. Her parents had assured her they only painted it in the first place because she loved fairy tales so much—not because they expected her to grow up and become a witch like them.

But was that true?

Anyway, she would make up for it now. She just wished it hadn't taken the end of the world to get here.

"When we were little," Maya said, breaking the silence, "you always said you wanted to be like her." She tilted her chin up at the painting. "But when we got older, you told me you didn't believe in magic anymore."

Hands clasped behind her back, Maya strode across the room and plopped onto the edge of the bed. In the window above her, a butterfly flitted by—no, not a butterfly, Cher realized with a second glance, but a pixie. It hovered outside, peering in at them with mild curiosity, before getting bored and gliding away.

"I told you so," Maya said, smirking.

Cher saw where this talk was going and gave a frustrated sigh. This wasn't just about magic.

It was about the breakup.

She had hoped they could just leave it in the past and focus instead on practicing a few beginner-level spells. Foolish of her to expect that, honestly. Magic was the reason they broke up. Of course they couldn't talk about one without bringing up the other.

"I'm sorry," she said, trying hard to keep calm. "I should have been more respectful of your beliefs—"

"Not 'beliefs.' *Knowledge.*" Maya sat forward, elbows on her knees. "Magic wasn't always this..." She searched for the right word. "It wasn't always this loud. But it was always there. Your parents weren't con-artists, you know."

Cher flinched at that. She'd called her parents con-artists on more than one occasion—whenever she tried making "normal" friends as a teenager. She'd never seen a ghost herself, not before the end of the world. For all she knew, they really were just lying about it all.

"And I wasn't just some kook making stuff up off the top of my head," Maya continued. "I always saw auras. I never asked you to 'believe' in my powers, just that you stop talking down to me whenever I—"

Her partner, still standing in the doorway, cleared her throat. "I'm gonna go, um, check on Alistair," she said, and ducked out of the attic.

Maya's eyes fluttered shut and she took a deep breath, forced a fresh smile.

"Anyway," she said, leveling her tone, "it isn't just me you owe an apology to. It's all the Coven Kids."

Cher frowned. She couldn't say Maya was wrong. After her thirteenth birthday, she'd ghosted all of them. The only reason she reconnected with Maya years later was because they ended up college roommates.

Their reunion had been an uncomfortable one, at least for Cher. Maya seemed enthusiastic and friendly enough, but Cher just couldn't shake off her old guilt so easily. Every time she looked at Maya, her mouth tasted sour and all she could think about was how she'd let her parents down, how Maya would have been a much better Olmstead than she was.

And despite their undeniable chemistry, there were times when she was paranoid Maya only wanted to get back in touch so she could convert her to the craft and boost the coven membership. She pestered Cher almost daily, begging her to visit the other Coven Kids with her.

"They miss you," she'd insisted. "No, really. They always ask about you."

After nearly a year together, which Cher spent making excuses not to hang out with the others, Maya gave up.

That is, until the Winter Solstice.

Cher came home from class that evening and paused at the door when she heard voices. She recognized her old friend Anton's nasally tone and turned right around, deciding to spend the night at her parents' house rather than face the Coven Kids.

Maya hadn't even warned her she would be hosting the party in their room. It was an ambush.

They fought the next day, when everyone was gone and Cher returned to the dorms. They hurled insults at each other.

They broke up.

"Did the others survive?" Cher asked now.

"Of course," said Maya. "Anton's got a trailer he parked near Derby Wharf lighthouse while shit was going down. Whatever protective spell your parents put on this house, he must have used too. Most other cars got swept out to sea, but his trailer was fine. I don't think he expected the spell to hold. He sounded so relieved when we last talked to him."

She waved a hand vaguely in the direction of the staircase, where her partner had disappeared. "Juliet and I weren't so lucky. Our house burned down, and that's how we ended up here. So did Nat and Sara's apartment. They're safe though, laying low and camping in a tent not too far from Anton."

"I heard those two ended up married."

Maya nodded. "I got hitched too." She held up her left hand and showed a golden wedding band. "Not legally, of course. Thanks to, y'know. Dear ol' President Bates and his promises to return America to the 'Golden Age.'"

They both rolled their eyes.

"Do you think he died?" Cher asked. "When the world ended?"

"I fucking hope so."

Their shared laughter felt like old times. It felt healing.

"Jules and I had a little ceremony in our backyard," Maya said, once their laughs subsided. "Sara officiated."

Cher's heart skipped a few beats as it cracked. "That's nice. Congratulations," she said, and she meant it.

She *was* happy for them. It was just a little bittersweet.

A silence descended for a while as she turned and examined the mural again, losing herself momentarily in the witch's garden. Strange, the resemblance the world outside bore to that fairy tale scene now.

"Why did you decide not to follow in your parents' footsteps?" Maya finally asked. "You don't have to tell me if you don't want to talk about it. It's just—I've sorta always wondered." It was the one topic they'd tip-toed around the whole year they dated. "Out of all of us, you were so into the craft when we were little. You couldn't wait to turn thirteen."

Cher shrugged. "That's a big decision to put on a kid," she said. "You know what it was like, being raised by witches. Other kids gave us such a hard time."

"Mm-hmm," Maya said. "I'll never forget the time we called your mom crying after Billy Parker's pool party. You remember that?"

"When Billy said his priest uncle blessed the pool water?"

"And everyone said it would burn us because we were witches."

"Yeah, and then they all ganged up on us and threw us in before we had even changed into our suits. How could I forget that? It was kinda traumatizing."

Maya's lip curled. "Those kids were such assholes."

"Yeah, well," Cher said, "all of that got to me eventually. By the time I turned thirteen, all I wanted was to blend in. And as I got older...I don't know. I always say I don't care what other people think anymore, but I guess it isn't true. I wanted to stick to my guns. Even if I regretted my choice.

"After Bates got elected, I really did start thinking maybe magic didn't exist. If it did, there wouldn't be so much evil in the world. Right? Or at least, that's what I thought back then."

Maya gave her a sympathetic smile. "Whatever forces are at work in this universe," she sighed, "sometimes it seems like they're steering us down a dark path. But I do believe the magic we practice can make our world a better place. I mean, reading auras isn't the most amazing power, but it feels nice to help people sort out their emotions. And I'm sure your parents felt the same way about helping the dead find peace."

Cher thought of the thousands of lost souls wandering

Salem since the apocalypse, the way their eyes flashed whenever they realized she could see them.

Maybe she could carry on her parents' work and start putting those souls to rest, after she finished helping Ferry.

Smiling, she pressed her palm against the mural—and winced as a splinter caught on her skin. When she pulled her hand back, she looked down and saw the circle of scabs where Ferry had pricked her, sealing their deal.

Oh. Right.

She closed her fingers into a fist and dropped her hand back to her side, turning away from the mural.

Maya hadn't noticed anything wrong. "So, can I welcome you to the coven now?" she asked.

Cher plastered on a smile. "I can't stay long. Why don't we go downstairs? I'll tell you why I finally decided to become a witch."

Chapter Twelve

Cher didn't *lie* to Maya and Juliet. She just left out some tiny details.

As the three of them sat around the kitchen table with fresh cups of chai tea and some stale store-bought cookies, she told the others she'd been kicked out of her own apartment. She didn't tell them it was her ex-fiancé who held her at gunpoint and shoved her out the door with no shoes or food or water.

She told them she started seeing ghosts after the world ended, and realized maybe her parents' powers, inherent in her own blood, had awakened of their own accord.

She told them she had met her familiar while wandering by the Crane River; she did not tell them she had met him while planning to take her own life. Nor did she tell them he was a kelpie with a vicious thirst for revenge.

What she *did* tell them was her familiar knew of an old witch who could help her learn some spells. She told them everything about the Devourer and the way Evelyn Wyse had rescued them.

"Wyse?" said Juliet. "I've heard of her."

"Me too," said Maya. "Didn't she own that magic shop on Essex Street?"

"Yeah," said Juliet. "It shut down a couple years ago, remember? No warning. And Evelyn vanished. Everyone thought maybe she just passed away. Her obituary never showed up in the papers, but that wasn't too strange." Frowning, she turned and explained to Cher, "Evelyn was a hedge witch. Kept to herself mostly. Never had a coven, and had no family as far as anyone knew. But everyone knew *of* her."

Maya nodded. "She was powerful too, if the rumors were true."

"She told me she lost her magic."

"*What?*" both Maya and Juliet exclaimed.

And so Cher told them everything she had learned in Evelyn's glade, about the Devourer and the Salem ghosts and the hunters in Danvers, about how the old witch attacked her, and how she just barely escaped by summoning flames.

Maya gnawed at her lower lip. "I wonder what happened to her? The apocalypse made our magic stronger. So how did she lose hers?"

"Do you think what she told you was true?" Juliet asked, her eyes wide and worried. "About the ghosts? And the witch hunters? You really think we're heading for another witch hunt?"

"I'm on my way to Danvers to find out," Cher replied. "See if there's anything I can do to stop this before it gets any worse."

They met her declaration with an astounded silence.

She took a deep breath. "Before the world ended," she explained, "I gave up. Bates got to me, and I just...I just accepted everything sucked because of him and nothing would change. I couldn't do it anymore. I couldn't keep protesting, I couldn't keep resisting, I couldn't keep reading the news, I just—all I could do was keep my head down and work to pay rent."

Merely uttering Bates's name was enough to rekindle all the despair and grief she had felt under his reign. One glance at Maya and Juliet told her they felt the same; their jaws tightened, their shoulders tensed, and their spines seemed to bow under the weight of their dread.

Maya nodded sympathetically. "I get it," she said. "I was at my wit's end too."

Juliet reached over and took her wife's hand, squeezing it affectionately.

"I thought," Cher continued, "after the apocalypse happened, maybe those of us who were lucky enough to survive could start over. Live freely. Peacefully. The thought of living off the land, with no money or government to dictate our every move..."

"It's a terrifying thought, being completely on our own," said Juliet, "especially with all the new creatures running around." She tilted her head and smiled softly. "But it's kind of thrilling too, right?"

Cher nodded, then sighed. "When I heard about the witch hunters, I realized I was wrong. All this magic didn't fix everything like I thought it would. Or, at least, the evil didn't all die off like I hoped.

"History is going to repeat itself, at least one last time." She lifted her chin. "So, I realized I have a choice. I can either surrender—like I did when Bates took over the whole country—and let the hunters establish control over Salem, or, I can do something *now*, before they gain any traction."

"But you're just one witch," Maya said. "What exactly do you plan to do against an entire neighborhood of armed bigots and an angry mob of ghosts? I mean, we'll do whatever we can to help, but—"

"We'd be no use against the ghosts," Juliet interrupted, cutting Maya a sideways glare. Cher could tell she didn't approve of the offer to help. "We're not psychics, so we can't see them. And even if we got the rest of the coven to help fight off the hunters, there are only six of us altogether. How many are we up against?"

"I'm going to go find out," Cher said. "Look—I'm not asking for your help with any of that."

"Nonsense," said Maya. "Something like this can't be done alone—"

Juliet's frown deepened. "Maya."

Cher held up a hand to quiet them both. "It's not like I'm going into battle. Not yet, at least. I'm just going to sneak out to their base to get an idea of what's going on. If I need you once I come up with a plan, I'll come back." She looked at Maya, who was about to retort, and said, "I promise. All I need from you right now is to teach me how to control my powers, so I can protect myself from the ghosts. Then I'll be on my way. I brought this to help."

She fished inside her jacket and pulled out Evelyn's grimoire, dropping the thick book onto the table with a deep *thud*. Everyone's teacup rattled on its saucer.

"There's some stuff in there about speaking to the dead, protecting against psychic attacks, and exorcising spirits," she explained. "I think it will help with half of our problem, at least. If I can get rid of the ghosts—and maybe the Devourer too—then we only have to worry about the witch hunters."

"Whose spellbook is this?" Maya asked. "Your parents'?"

Cher shook her head. "I stole it. From Evelyn."

For the second time, the others both responded to her with stunned silence.

"It's not like she was using it," Cher said defensively. "I mean, she was, but she was using it as a reference to perform that blood ritual. It's kind of like an eye for an eye, right? Or whatever. She tried stealing my magic, so I stole hers. Or, well...what's left of it..."

The more she talked, the guiltier she felt. She could tell by how worn the book's cover was, how yellow its pages were, Evelyn had treasured it and worked hard on it for most of her long life.

"I need it more than she does," she finished weakly, trying to reassure herself as much as the others.

She cracked the spine open and flipped to page 166, the one labeled *Dealing with the Dead*. Two words caught her eye, written in dark, heavy strokes and underlined several times: *Summoning Spell*.

An idea struck her.

There were only two other psychics she knew who might help her learn more about her own psychic powers. Unfortunately, they were both deceased.

But what if she taught herself this summoning spell?

What if she could talk to her parents?

"Well, I'm sorry, but you can't use it," Maya said, interrupting Cher's thoughts. "A lot of witches put safeguards on their grimoires. If someone tries using it without the owner's permission, it could curse you."

"And a witch like Evelyn Wyse?" said Juliet. "She's sure to have something like that in place."

"But her magic's gone," Cher countered. "Couldn't that mean any spells she placed on this book are broken?"

Maya and Juliet exchanged a glance. They both shrugged uneasily.

"We don't know exactly how magic works anymore," Maya said eventually. "A lot of it is just as new to us as it is to you. Maybe using one of her spells will rebound on you. Maybe it won't. You think it's worth the risk?"

I'm dead anyway, Cher thought. A curse couldn't make her situation any worse.

She could tell which answer Maya and Juliet wanted her to give them, though. So, she let the book fall shut again, slumped back in her seat, and crossed her arms, feigning defeat.

"Fine," she said. "At least run me through the basics then. Please. I just need something I can build off of. Maybe—maybe all the psychic stuff will come naturally to me later on."

* * *

Before their lesson, Maya cooked up some rice and cream of mushroom soup. Cher's stomach had shrunk after nearly a week of little to no real food; she doled herself only one scoop of the rice and felt bloated and sleepy after eating only half of it.

Sitting at the kitchen table with her half-eaten meal in front of her, she jiggled her leg up and down and waited for the others to finish eating. If they didn't hurry up, she was afraid she might slip into a food coma right at the table, and she had the feeling once she fell asleep, she'd be out indefinitely. The last couple of days were finally catching up with her, and she desperately needed a recharge.

But first, magic lessons. And, after that, she would have to hold out just a little longer until Maya and Juliet went to bed, so she could experiment with the contents of Evelyn's grimoire in peace. She'd sleep better knowing how to control her powers and fend off ghosts.

The cat, Alistair, came strolling into the kitchen as they ate. With the prospect of a meal, it appeared he'd forgotten all about his stranger danger. He rubbed against Cher's legs and released a demanding yowl.

Juliet stood and fished a can of cat food from the kitchen cupboards. As she scraped a third of the wet food into a little porcelain dish, she explained to Cher how Alistair must have belonged to the old woman who bought the house from the Olmsteads. If she'd survived the end of the world, she wasn't home when it happened, and she hadn't returned yet. Alistair latched onto Maya and Juliet the second they showed up, lonely and needy as a baby.

Luckily, his previous owner had the cupboards stocked with a few crates of canned cat food.

"What'll you do when we run out of this, mister?" Juliet said, nudging the cat with a toe. "It won't last forever. Better brush up on your hunting skills."

Alistair growled, and then growled even lower when everyone laughed.

"You know," said Maya conversationally, after gulping down another mouthful of rice, "your aura's changed, Cher."

Cher stopped shaking her leg. "Oh? Is that a thing?"

Shrugging, Maya said, "It happens. People grow. Their moods and intentions and dreams shift."

"What color was it before?"

"When we met again in college," Maya explained, "it was gray." Her smile was sad.

"I take it that isn't a good color."

"It's not *necessarily* bad. If it has a silver gleam to it, it can mean you're in a time of reflection and healing. But yours was dull and faint, almost hard to see sometimes, especially near—well, near the end of our relationship. Gray usually signals depression. I think a lot of us had a little gray in our auras when Bates was in power, so I wasn't so surprised about it. Though, judging by what you said earlier, it got even worse for you the last few years."

"Yeah."

"I'm sorry."

"It's not your fault," Cher said. "I know I should have been seeing a therapist. I just couldn't afford it."

"I get that." After another bite of her rice, Maya added, "I'm just happy you got your color back, is all."

"Got it back?"

"Sure. Don't you remember asking me to read everyone's auras when we were little?" Maya asked. "We were, oh...probably eleven or twelve? And the five of us were right upstairs in the attic."

Cher strained to remember, but truth be told, living the last decade in survival mode had turned her happier memories into shambles, both short- and long-term. There was never time to sit and reminisce; it was all work, all the time.

But now she thought about it, she did vaguely

remember being a little jealous of Maya, who claimed her powers manifested more than a year before her thirteenth birthday.

Right—now she remembered. Maya admitted she could already see people's auras, just like her mother. Anton said he didn't believe her and got Nat and Sara riled up too.

It was Cher who asked Maya to prove it by reading everyone's auras right then and there.

Even after she told everyone what colors they were, Anton accused her of lying. It was their first big fight, and Maya hadn't spoken to them for a few weeks, until they all begged her forgiveness by putting their arcade tickets together to buy her the biggest stuffed dragon behind the counter.

"Wait, you weren't just making up colors for everyone?" Cher said.

Laughing, Maya smacked her arm. "No, you jerk! I was telling the truth."

"You said mine was purple, with a little yellow around the edges." Cher snapped her fingers as the memory came rushing back to her in more detail. "Purple because of all the psychic energy stored up in me. Yellow because I was always smiling."

"Well." Maya sobered up a bit. "Maybe. But that was near your thirteenth birthday. Yellow can symbolize optimism *or* indecision. Now I'm wondering if maybe that was when your skepticism started kicking in."

Cher's smile faded. "Oh," she said. "Probably." She picked up her spoon and picked at the last of her dinner, though she didn't eat any more. "So, what color am I now?"

"Purple again," Maya said, her face brightening. "Even more striking than it used to be."

"And the yellow?"

"Gone." Maya finished eating and pushed her bowl away. "Replaced by a bright white. That means only one thing: you found balance. You know where you belong in this world. You are genuinely, truly, as happy as can be."

The truth of her words struck hard.

It was too bad Ferry wasn't around to hear. *I told you so, Olmstead,* he'd say. *You don't want to die after all.*

She didn't, no. If she could keep on living like this, she wouldn't mind it at all. She might even thrive in this world if she were given the chance.

But she'd long since accepted her fate. Anyway, Ferry probably couldn't wait to be rid of her.

Juliet stood and cleared everyone's plates, taking them out the back door to wash in a bucket. Alistair followed, leaping onto the wide ledge outside the window and sprawling out in the fresh air, full and content.

"Ready?" Maya asked Cher.

"Yes," she replied with a sigh of relief. "I've been waiting for this moment for a long time."

"Me too." Grinning, she stood and beckoned Cher to follow her into the living room.

* * *

They sat on the floor across from one another at the coffee table. Maya folded her hands on the tabletop and sat with her spine straight. Cher, meanwhile, leaned back casually with her palms flat against the floor. Truth be told, she was nervous, but she didn't want to show it.

"I'm going to tell you word-for-word what my godfather taught me," Maya said, then cleared her throat and recited, "'Magic is a matter of will. No potion or spell is complete without a dose of the witch's willpower. Desire and need are powerful forces, and dangerous too. Therefore, it is important for a witch to learn to control their magic, so their spells do not exceed their intentions or expectations.'"

Cher thought back to the fireball incident inside Evelyn's cave, the burning in her gut that spread through her veins and out her fingertips.

She explained those sensations to Maya and asked, "Does it always hurt so bad?"

"Not at all," Maya assured her. "It isn't supposed to, at least. I mean, I've never cast an elemental spell before, like your fireball. Elementalists were always the rarest type of witches, and usually their powers were more subtle. They might have a green thumb, or an uncanny ability to start a fire even with very little supplies. Unless they couldn't control their magic, in which case—worst case scenario—they might spontaneously combust."

Cher's eyes widened. "Lucky that didn't happen to me, I guess," she said. "But does that mean I'm an elementalist as well? Not just a psychic?"

Maya unclasped her hands and looked down at her palms. "Y'know, I've been wondering…. Hold tight."

She stood and strolled back into the kitchen, calling for Juliet.

"What is it?" Juliet called from the back porch.

"We got any seeds?"

She returned to the living room a few seconds later with a packet of sunflower seeds. Juliet followed and, like a bright orange shadow, Alistair trailed right behind her.

"Here. I want us all to try something out."

Maya fished a seed out of the packet and tossed it to Cher, who caught it in cupped hands. Then she shook two more seeds into her palm and passed one to Juliet, and they took their seats at either end of the coffee table. Alistair curled up in Juliet's lap.

A thrill crept down Cher's spine. She had a feeling she knew where this was going.

"Okay," said Maya. "Everyone, close your eyes. Tap into your willpower, deep in your core. Feel the fire of your energy and sink into it. Let it drip into your veins."

Her voice was deep and soothing, like a meditation guide. "Now, envision yourself holding a sunflower. Imagine the seed cracking open, the sunflower sprouting gradually, the roots tickling your fingers. Imagine the exchange of oxygen and carbon dioxide as you breathe life into this tiny seed. Imagine the bright shades of yellow and green, the earthy brown in the center..."

Cher felt her sunflower seed dance in her palm, and her lips stretched into a peaceful smile.

Then there came a sudden *pop* and a *zip*, and something smacked her lightly across the face.

She yelped and snapped her eyes open to see nothing but sunflower petals. Somewhere behind all that yellow, Maya and Juliet were cracking up.

"I said '*gradually!*'" Maya said, wiping tears of laughter from her eyes.

"Whoops." Cher took the sunflower by its stem and laid it gently across the table. It was about the length of her forearm, its petals bright and beautiful.

Her magic did that. *She* did that.

She glanced at the others and saw that they, too, had

made some progress, both holding half-sprouted seeds in their hands. They looked just as excited as she felt.

"So we *can* all practice elemental magic then," said Maya. "Just as I thought."

She shut her eyes and finished growing her sunflower, then leaned across the table to give the finished product to Juliet with a flourish. "M'lady."

Juliet giggled and tickled Maya's nose with the sunflower's petals.

"But we still each have specialties," Cher said. "Neither of you can see ghosts. I can't see auras."

"Right," said Juliet. "Why do you think that is?"

Maya nibbled thoughtfully on a fresh sunflower seed. "I'm not sure," she said. "I always thought elementalism was a specialized branch of magic too. Maybe it wasn't."

"Maybe it was just beyond our skill before," said Juliet. "And now the world is so charged with magic, it's more accessible."

"Or maybe," said Cher, "we were so out-of-touch with the earth and the universe and ourselves, tapping into this kind of power was too difficult for most modern witches."

Juliet stood and reached for two books on top of the fireplace's mantel. She handed one to Maya. Each had a pencil tucked between the pages, and as Juliet sat back down, both women opened their books to a blank page and started scribbling down some notes.

Their grimoires. Cher felt a pang of envy; not for the first time, she wished she had a book of her own to record everything she had learned about the new world.

Though she supposed there was no point in starting one, if she would be kelpie food soon enough.

After a moment, Juliet said, "You know, I think you're

right. I think maybe elementalism requires a connection to the world most of us were missing in the twenty-first century."

"That's right," said Maya, her eyes lighting up as she connected dots. "This type of magic was much more common centuries ago, when more people lived off the land and worked closely with the earth. Amazing..."

She tapped her pencil against her lips and continued to jot down her thoughts.

The hair on Cher's arms stood on end as another shiver of excitement passed through her. This was what she'd been missing out on all these years. This sense of belonging and growth, alongside people who shared her passion to understand the way the world worked.

A twinge of sadness dampened her smile.

Better late than never, she told herself.

"Hey," she said, holding out her hand. "Pass me the seeds. I want to try that again. *Gradually* this time."

Ferry had paced around the flooded neighborhood some six times now, so deep in thought he barely noticed he was walking in circles around the ruined blocks. He'd been strolling half the day, stopping now and then to dip his snout into the ocean water swirling around his ankles and sooth his dry, rotting flesh. It felt nice enough, but he much preferred freshwater to saltwater.

He could not stand another moment with Charity Olmstead. Perhaps he would call off their mission and devour her the moment he returned to her. Or perhaps he wouldn't return to her at all. Perhaps he would go home to the Crane River instead and pretend the last few days had never happened.

Better yet, he could fetch his spawn and get them both the hell out of Salem. Enough with this place. It had brought him nothing but trouble.

Yes, leaving sounded like a good idea. He would return home for the night, fetch his spawn in the morning, and the two of them could leave Salem and its problems for the humans to handle.

Though that meant he would fail to avenge his mate.

Surely she would understand. Charity was just too insufferable to work with, and useless with magic to boot. He doubted she could really help him get his revenge anyway.

But as he turned towards home, his new plan just refused to sit well.

Perhaps he wouldn't leave Salem. Perhaps he could find *another* witch, one more experienced than Charity, who could take him straight to Danvers so they could wreak havoc upon his mate's murderers. A witch who wouldn't need to waste all this time learning the basics, because they had already mastered their spell-craft long ago.

And it would have to be a witch who wouldn't spew any of this nonsense about *familiars.*

Ferry strolled out of the neighborhood and passed the crumbled arcade. He kept walking until he reached the edge of the forest, half a mile or so from Charity's childhood home.

Turning back, he heaved a sigh and muttered, "Farewell, Miss Olmstead. Good luck. I am calling off our contract. Live long and happy."

From the corner of his eye he saw the gemstone in his saddle drip blood. Charity's blood. It slid down the leather and fell into the water.

He sniffed the air. Relief washed over him as he realized he could no longer smell Charity's scent. The contract had truly ended. Their bond was broken.

Ferry was free.

So why did he feel so sad? Why did he still want to turn around and return to her side, as if a thread connected them and tugged him back in her direction?

Shaking those thoughts away, he lifted a hoof and prepared to step back into the forest. His cracked hoof hooked in midair and froze.

"Dammit!"

He couldn't do it. He couldn't leave her.

Chapter Thirteen

Cher practiced growing seeds for the rest of the afternoon and well into the evening. Maya and Juliet took a break to prepare a small dinner, but Cher was still full from lunch and, anyway, she wanted to perfect the sunflower trick before the sun went down.

The more she practiced, the more she understood how her willpower worked, how to ride it like a wave, how to contain it before it slipped out of her control.

By the time the sun set, she was so high on her own magic she was sure she could pull off the summoning spell from Evelyn's grimoire. If all went according to plan, she'd be reunited with her late parents in just a few hours.

"We're wiped," Maya said. "Jules and I are gonna get some sleep. Need anything?"

"Nope, I'm all set," Cher said, sticking yet another sunflower into a vase Maya had found stored away in the kitchen cupboards. It was nearly full now. "Think I'll stay up just a little longer."

Maya looked concerned. "Okay, but don't wear yourself out," she warned. "You can make yourself sick if you use too much energy. Like a magical hangover."

Cher laughed, but Maya didn't.

"Anyway, didn't you say you needed to get some real rest before hitting the road?"

"I did. I *do*." Admittedly, exhaustion hummed steadily beneath the adrenaline rush of spell-casting, and Cher did feel a little nauseous. "But I also want to make sure I'm ready to defend myself out there if I have to. I promise I won't be up much longer, *Mom*."

She smirked at her own joke, but Maya's frown didn't falter.

"Alright. Well, see you tomorrow. Don't forget to blow out the candles when you're done."

"Of course. Goodnight."

She didn't mention she would be gone by sunrise; that Ferry was coming to fetch her before the others woke up.

Instead she said, "Hey, Maya? Thanks for your help."

Maya gave a humble nod. "It's been great catching up, Cher," she said. "I'm happy you're here."

Then she disappeared down the hallway, leaving Cher fidgeting with the packet of sunflower seeds, biding her time.

Eventually Juliet came out of the kitchen, muttered a quick "g'night," and followed her wife to bed. Alistair trailed behind her, pausing at the bedroom door to glare over his shoulder.

Did he know what she was planning?

No. Of course not. He was probably just annoyed she hadn't left yet.

Once the coast was clear, she lifted her jacket from the

couch where she'd tossed it and pulled Evelyn's grimoire out from underneath it.

The book felt heavier to her than it had earlier. Hopefully it was only her imagination, and not an ominous sign.

She carried her jacket, the grimoire, and the three-armed candelabra upstairs to the attic, away from any prying eyes. The candlelight cast flickering, jumping shadows up and down the narrow stairwell with each step she took. She'd spent a third of her life in this house and never once felt as jumpy and afraid as she did now.

But what if Maya and Juliet were right? What if she brought a curse down on herself by using Evelyn's grimoire? What if she was about to bite off more than she could chew and try a spell way beyond her skill level?

What if, instead of summoning her parents, she summoned a demon?

She shook her imagination clean.

I'll follow each step carefully, she reassured herself. *I'll reread every single word Evelyn wrote in the instructions three or four times, so I don't mess anything up. I can do this. I am an Olmstead. I am an Olmstead. I am an Olmstead....*

Stepping into her old bedroom eased some of her fears. The moon shone in through the window over her bed, casting a circle on the floor and splashing a silver streak across the mural. Bits of dust sparkled in the moonlight.

It felt safe. It felt like a room made for magic.

Cher tossed her jacket on the bed, set the candles on her nightstand, and took a seat in the middle of the moonlit circle. She cracked the grimoire open like a child taking a sneak-peek at her hidden Christmas presents.

Instead of skipping straight to the summoning spell,

she took her time, reverently turning each individual page and scanning her eyes across Evelyn's handwriting. The book was brimming with useful information. Why skip over it all? Maybe she would find something she didn't know she needed.

She skimmed lists of potion ingredients, love spells, elemental spells, spells meant to boost crystal charges. There were rough sketches of herbs and talismans and runes in many of the margins. The grimoire was a treasure trove—more comprehensive than even the most advanced guides to witchcraft Cher remembered seeing on her parents' old bookshelves.

Even when she came to the summoning spell, she turned past it, instead looking for pages to dog-ear for later reference.

The deeper she got into the book, the hastier and less legible were Evelyn's scribbles—and the darker and more difficult the spells became. The word "blood" appeared often, and Cher remembered the cold edge of Evelyn's knife against her throat.

But these weren't all evil and nefarious spells. For every blood ritual that promised more power, there were well-intentioned uses, such as enhanced health potions and protective runes.

She lingered over those runes, sketched under a heading that read *Illusions*. One of the illusory spells—a ward—claimed it could turn anything, whether small as a button or big as a house, invisible to anyone besides the spellcaster, unless the witch revealed the location to them.

"A whole house, huh?" she muttered to herself, then looked at the room around her.

She would feel much better about leaving Maya and

Juliet if she knew the witch hunters could never find them. The house was its own peaceful world, but each time she glanced out the windows she was afraid she would see an angry mob marching to burn everything to the ground and hang her and the others for witchcraft. If she could guarantee that wouldn't happen....

As she read through the instructions, her hope faded. The spell was way beyond her skill level, and for larger objects—such as a house—it required at least five witches.

Five witches, like the Coven Kids and Juliet.

She crawled over to her old nightstand and fished through the drawers until she found a dull pencil.

Above the spell's instructions she wrote, "Maya: Please try this. I'm begging you. Stay safe."

Then she ripped the page out of Evelyn's grimoire and left it on the nightstand for Maya to find in the morning. Maybe, just maybe, Maya and Juliet would throw caution to the wind and use the spell, even if it was torn out of a stolen grimoire.

Satisfied, Cher returned to her spot on the floor and finally opened to page 166.

"Alright," she whispered. "Let's do this."

Evelyn's grimoire mentioned a few techniques for summoning spirits. The simplest required drawing a complete circle to limit the spirit's movement, and another protective circle around the witch in case the first one somehow failed.

Cher had no chalk. But there was salt in the kitchen downstairs.

A few moments later, she stood in the attic with a box of salt in one hand and the grimoire in the other.

The instructions called for a blessing of the circle as it was drawn, and so she recited the words under her breath as she tipped the box's contents onto the floor. "May this circle offer me protection from psychic danger, and bind any ghost summoned within its force field so that no harm will befall me."

Careful not to disturb her artwork, she stepped over that circle and traced a second circle, then she sat cross-legged in the middle and set the grimoire in front of her.

The next step read, "Focus your gaze on the opposite circle and state your intention to summon the spirit into that space. Be sure to name the spirit fully and clearly."

Cher took a deep breath and turned her attention back to the empty circle across from her.

What felt like hours passed before she was ready to speak the summoning. She read and reread the instructions, then reread them again. She double-checked the circles for any gaps. She pushed aside her weariness and dug deep inside herself for her willpower, like a pitcher winding up for the throw.

The room was cold, and she had a feeling it would only get colder with the presence of ghosts. Perhaps she was only stalling, but she stood and fetched her jacket from the bed, returned to her seat, and fidgeted with the zipper for a few more moments.

Then finally, "I call to the circle," she said in a sharp, commanding whisper, "Roslyn Miriam Olmstead and Theodore John Olmstead."

Her eyes drifted closed as the breeze outside whistled

around the house, sending a shiver down the back of her neck.

She tried stirring up the memory of her parents' voices calling her name, as if they were just downstairs, "Cher-bear, dinner's ready."

She thought of all she wanted to say to them; imagined how they would react when she told them about the whales.

Her heart swelled. With hope, with magic, with love.

When she opened her eyes, smiling through her joyous tears and eager to welcome her parents, the circle was empty.

Her smile dropped.

"I call to the circle," she tried again, a little louder this time, and with stronger intention despite her shaking voice, "Roslyn Miriam Olmstead and Theodore John Olmstead."

She did not close her eyes. She did not even blink. The breeze blew harder and turned into a gust of wind. Cher strained to listen, hoping she might pick her mother and father's whispers out of the noise.

Nothing.

"Mom? Dad?" she said into the dark, sitting perfectly still as if that played any part in the ritual.

A big drop of rain smacked against the window, making her flinch. A downpour began. Lightning flashed, highlighting the empty circle across from her, and thunder rumbled in the distance.

Alone. Cher was alone.

She drew her knees up to her chest and wept.

* * *

When the tears were finally out of her system, she stood and tip-toed back down the stairs, returning to the attic after she found a broom and dustpan.

"What a waste of salt," she sniffled to herself, as she started cleaning up her mess.

She wasn't only upset her summoning spell failed; she missed her parents more than ever before, and she only realized it when she opened her eyes and didn't find them waiting to greet her.

As soon as the last of the salt was swept into the dustpan, she fell into a crouch, squeezed her eyes shut, and let herself cry some more. The storm raged outside, clouds blocking out the moonlight.

Exhaustion caught up to her after a while. She yawned between sobs, rubbed her eyes dry with her palms—and froze when she noticed the scabs on her hand, where Ferry had pricked her and sealed their contract, were gone.

They couldn't have healed already. Frowning, she held her hand closer to the candlelight to get a better look. But there was nothing there, not even the hint of an injury.

Before she could wonder what was going on, the candles winked out, all three at once, sending her into utter darkness.

Her blood turned cold.

"Forgetting something?" a man's voice said in her ear, and she shrieked as something fell with a *thud* onto the nightstand in front of her.

Lightning flashed outside, illuminating the room long enough for Cher to spot a ghostly pale finger pointing at the last instruction for the summoning spell: "Do NOT forget to deactivate and close your circles after your ritual is complete."

The room went dark again, then the man read aloud: *"'Failure to deactivate a circle may be taken as an open invitation.'* Huh."

Another flash of lightning. Cher got a clear look at the man, at his gray face under a powdered wig.

He flashed a grin even more demonic than Ferry's and lunged.

Chapter Fourteen

C harity awoke to a pain between her eyes so severe, she immediately sat up and vomited what little was in her stomach onto the floor.

Wherever she was, it was too dark to see. Lifting a hand to wipe bits of undigested apple skin and rice away from her lips, she discovered her wrists and ankles were bound together by heavy shackles nailed to the brick wall behind her.

Her gut roiled again, threatening to send up more puke, but she managed to swallow it down. She was sitting on a lumpy mattress, one she guessed might be stuffed with hay, on a flimsy wooden frame low to the ground and groaning under her weight. She felt around for a pillow but as far as she could tell there was none. There was also no blanket, or even a window to tell her what time of night or day it might be.

Her jacket was gone, her extra apples and Evelyn's grimoire with it. Someone had changed Cher's dirty night-gown for a fresh, thin cotton shift that fell to her ankles like something her grandmother might wear, and her hair had been washed and combed. Her feet were still bare, but soft and clean.

Something light tickled her collarbone. She reached up and brushed her fingers against a plastic zip-tie, loose around her neck.

She had no memory of what had happened after the ghost attacked her, no memory of coming here, no memory of being groomed, or locked up like a recaptured stray.

And that made her sick again.

"*Tsk.*"

Cher tensed at the sound of someone's voice from across the room. There came a scratch and a crackle as the stranger lit a match and touched it to a candle's wick. Her eyes adjusted to the new light and the whole room turned upside-down as she recognized her captor standing in the doorway.

"That won't do," said Nora Winston—the woman who, once upon a time, was nearly Cher's mother-in-law. "Here."

She set the candle down on a table in the center of the room. Then she slipped a backpack off her shoulder and fished out a bottle of mouthwash.

Tossing it to Cher, she said, "Wash up. You need to look your best for your trial. We can't have everyone thinking we mistreat our guests. We aren't barbarians."

"T-trial?" Cher was too confused, too stunned to be angry. Mindlessly, she obeyed Nora's order and rinsed the stale taste from her mouth.

She had a feeling she knew exactly where she was and what was happening, but whenever she reached for explanations, trying to connect the dots in her mind, every coherent thought flitted teasingly away from her.

"Of course." Nora examined her nails, nonchalant. "You didn't think you could just come waltzing into our home screaming threats without consequence, did you?"

"What?" The bottle of mouthwash slipped from her fingers and spilled across the hardwood floor. "Threats?"

"Oh, come on!" Nora gestured to the mess. "Pick that up. Now! Hurry, before it all spills. What a waste." When her orders went ignored, she barked, "*Now!*"

Cher jumped, stretching and straining awkwardly to pick up the mouthwash, but the chains held her back.

"Pathetic," Nora snarled, and retrieved the bottle herself. "The cap." She held out a hand. Cher held the cap out to her, but she refused to come any closer. "Throw it to me."

She did and the cap landed neatly in Nora's outstretched palm.

"I don't understand. What's going on? Where am I?"

Danvers. That much she'd gathered the second Nora had mentioned a trial. But how did she get here? When had she threatened anyone? None of this made any sense.

Nora picked up the candle and turned her back, ignoring the questions as she moved to exit the room and leave Cher alone again. She halted only because someone else stood in the doorway now, blocking her way out.

Dean.

"What are you doing here?" Nora asked, an edge of panic in her voice. "I thought I told you to get a patrol together."

"I sent Ava out instead," Dean replied, taking a further step into the room. Nora obstructed him. "I'm here to see her."

"It isn't safe for you—"

He shoved past his mother, the candle's flame flickering violently with the sudden movement.

"Dean!" Nora snapped, digging her nails into his shoulder. "Stop it!"

He shrugged her off and crouched before Cher, who trembled and yanked her hands away from him even as he tried to hold them.

Nora grabbed the candle and ran out the door, calling for help and leaving Dean and Cher without any light. His fingers finally found hers and refused to let go. He was shaking as badly as she was.

"I won't let this happen to you," he said, touching his forehead to hers.

She wanted to pull away, repulsed by him. He'd stooped low when he kicked her out of her own apartment, but *this?* This was a whole new level of evil.

"This is why you told me to get out of Salem?" she said, everything snapping into place. "You knew. You knew all along this was happening. And you didn't tell me."

"How could I?" he said, grunting as she pulled her hands free and pushed him away. He took the hint and shifted away from her. "When my father said he wanted to build a community for survivors, I thought—I thought he'd finally changed."

Cher laughed.

"He sent me and my mother out to scout for places where we could set up outposts."

"And that's why you took the apartment," she said.

"Right." He had the decency to sound ashamed of himself at least. "But before she and I left, I overheard her talking to my father about their plans for the town. He was building a second area a couple of miles north for 'business,' as he called it. And he had a name for our little community, 'the Court.' The place where we all live, he hoped to name 'Oyer.' The second area—"

"'Terminer,'" Cher said, the word foul in her throat.

A community named for the very court that conducted the original Salem witchcraft trials, the Court of Oyer and Terminer.

Of course. It was happening all over again.

"Yeah," Dean said. "Exactly. I took a walk up there while my mother rounded up a group to go scouting with us, and I saw the gallows."

"Why? What does your father get out of this?"

"I don't know. Some sick pleasure. A power trip. But, Cher, please—when I saw your apartment still standing, believe me, I prayed you were long gone. Somewhere safe and far away. Like you somehow already knew all this was going on. While my mother and our scouts came up with a plan of attack in case you were still living there, I sneaked off on my own."

"Then you answered the door."

Shouts and thundering footsteps sounded outside.

"I was too ashamed," he said, speaking quickly and quietly. "Ashamed of myself for believing my father had changed. Ashamed of my own blood."

The door banged open and candlelight encircled the room. Dean stood hurriedly, looming over Cher.

"Trust me," he whispered.

And suddenly, before she could even scoff, he had her by the throat and was shouting at her.

"*You monster!*" His breath was hot against her face. She tried shoving him off, but her arms were pinned beneath his knees, his fingers loose around her neck. "You thought you could trick me? Joke's on you."

He let her go and tightened the zip-tie around her neck —not enough to strangle her, but enough to send a flash of panic through her.

She froze in fear. Instinctively she reached into her core, trying to tap into her magic and break her bonds, to fight free of this place the same way she'd broken out of Evelyn's caves.

But her insides were ice cold. There was no magic there.

"Your evil spells won't work on me anymore." He bared his teeth in a snarl, but his eyes were wide, his gaze pointed. He tapped a finger against the zip-tie once, twice.

Then it hit her. *He's acting.* Trying to let her in on a secret without letting his mother know he was giving away their tactics.

The zip-tie. Plastic—a relic from the old, miserable world before magic was free and untamed.

It blocked her energy. She had to find a way to get it off.

"Now, now, Dean," Nora cooed from the doorway, stepping into the room behind the guards who had swarmed in ahead of her. "There will be plenty of time for retribution at tonight's trial. Don't hurt her. Yet."

Satisfaction oozed from her smirk. Cher wanted to spit at her.

One of the guards brandished an iron poker, another a knife. They grabbed Dean's arms and pulled him off Cher, but they didn't keep their weapons trained on *him.*

"Assholes," she muttered. As if she were any threat to them, all chained up as she was.

She snapped her teeth at them, just for the hell of it —*might as well play into the game Dean was playing, right?*—and received an answer in the form of the flat side of the iron poker striking her across the jaw.

It would bruise. Fast. She could already feel her lower lip swelling.

Dean gave her a pleading look as the guards guided him away from her. His arm twitched, as if with the impulse to throw the guards away from him and rush to Cher's side.

But he refrained. Just as quickly as it appeared, the desperation was gone, replaced with fake fury. Or perhaps it wasn't fake at all. Perhaps he was only directing it at her for the sake of the act, when in truth he was furious with his own mother and father.

"I'll see you soon," he promised, adding a dash of menace to his tone.

Then he was gone with the guards, leaving Cher alone with Nora. Her almost-mother-in-law smiled insincerely and tilted her head to one side.

"I knew it," she said. "He never really loved you."

She took a step closer to the bed, leaving the candle on the table again so her face was cast in shadow.

"You had your claws in him deep, didn't you? How long he was under that spell of yours?" She lifted her chin. "Well. No more. Checkmate, Charity Olmstead. It'll be fun watching you swing."

Before Cher could come up with a retort, Nora was gone with her candle, darkness falling back over the cell.

Chapter Fifteen

C harity worked at the zip-tie for what must have been hours, tugging and scraping and picking until her nails broke and the plastic cut through the skin of her fingers and palms. Her hands wouldn't stop shaking. She felt so weak and hungry, and she wondered how long ago she'd been captured.

Ferry will save me, she thought, trying to calm herself down. Any second now he would come galloping through camp with a whole army of kelpies, if that was what it would take to save her—if not for her own sake, then for the sake of revenge.

Her blood. He had taken her blood. It was how kelpies tracked their prey, he'd said. Even if he hadn't been there when she was captured, he could just follow the scent of her blood.

Except the mark wasn't there anymore. Did that mean he couldn't trail her anymore?

No. No, he would save her. He had to.

She tried one last time to get a fingernail under the

locking bar of the zip-tie and pry herself free. But her finger slipped, and the plastic cut into the skin under her nail. She shoved the finger into her mouth to stop the bleeding.

The door burst open and in strode the two guards from before. The one with the knife held a burlap sack and some rope in his hands. While the woman with the poker pointed her weapon at Cher, the man threw the sack over her head and knotted the rope around it.

The clink of iron sounded, and the shackles fell away from Cher's ankles. She expected the same to happen to the ones around her wrists. But those remained. Instead, someone removed the chain from the wall and tugged it, leading her out of the room and up sloping ground.

When it finally evened out, she heard a door creak open and smelled fresh air through the burlap.

The guard who held her chain tugged hard, while the one at her back nudged her forward with the poker. She took a blind, hobbling step forward, unable to tell if it was day or night. A stone sliced into the bottom of her foot and she stumbled. The guard at her back barked at her to stand up, keep moving.

After a few more steps, she realized she had an audience.

"That's her," someone said in a scandalized half-whisper. "The one who tried attacking people in the square the other day."

"What a monster."

"I heard she tried killing the Mayor's wife and son last week. Hexed the building they were camping in, and it collapsed on them. They were lucky to escape."

"I heard she bewitched Dean Winston even before the world ended."

"Weren't they engaged?"

"Against his will, it sounds like."

Wrong.

"They met at a bar."

That much was true. She'd been nursing the big breakup with Maya—still, after nearly six months apart—and Dean saw her crying into a glass of rum and coke. He took the drink from her and dragged her onto the dance floor, insisting she cheer up.

"Supposedly she spiked his drink with some kind of potion."

That was not true. Not at all. The two of them were so busy dancing and yelling to each other over the music they forgot to stop at the bar and order more drinks.

"Probably just after his money."

Again, not true. Cher didn't even learn who Dean's family were until a few days after they met, and in fact—when she discovered his father was the most corrupt mayor in Salem's history—she considered dumping him.

But, by then, she was already falling in love. His personal politics were nothing like his father's, thank God, though she'd wished Dean could see Bernard for the crook he really was.

All it boiled down to was Dean made her laugh. He brought her joy. That was really all that mattered to her back then.

"Or maybe she was planning to take over Salem." Someone clicked their tongue. "It would've been a clever scheme, getting close to the Mayor like that by marrying into his family. Who knows what kind of world we'd be living in if she had pulled it off?"

"Who knows if we'd even be alive? She probably would've murdered us all."

"Seems like she tried to do that anyway."

"You think she ended the world?"

"Oh yeah, definitely."

"Out of spite?"

"No, not necessarily. I think she would have done it whether she married Dean or not. That was her plan all along. But she failed. Both times, lucky for us. First when Dean broke off the engagement, and again when the world changed. She didn't think she'd get caught. Didn't think any of us would survive. We did though, and now she'll have to pay the price."

Cher would have laughed at the absurdity of their delusions, but then she heard another voice—a child's.

"Let me see, Mommy!" A little boy. "Let me see the witch. Are they going to burn her?"

"I hope so," the mother replied.

"I think they'll hang her like the others," another child chimed in.

"But that's too quick. She's not like the rest. She's worse. They'll make sure she suffers," said an adult, as if to reassure the children.

Only then did the reality of the situation strike Cher and shake her to the core.

She was going to die. And these people would cheer it on all the way.

"*Witch.*"

This voice was closer, so close it seemed to echo in her

mind. It was a voice she recognized, a ghost's voice, the last voice she'd heard in the attic before blacking out.

Had he somehow brought her to Danvers?

"Wi-iiitch," the ghost teased, *"you're going to die now."*

History repeating. And she was powerless to stop it.

The guards dragged and prodded her for an eternity, forcing her on and on over a dirt-and-pebble path. More than once she stubbed a toe or rolled an ankle, and each time her captors yanked her back up to her feet.

The voices of the onlookers remained all the while at her back, and she could hear shuffling footsteps. The audience was following her. They wanted to see her trial. They wanted front row seats to the spectacle.

The guard at her back shouted a loud, sudden greeting. Someone shouted back, and then she heard heavy gates creaking open. A tug of her chain jerked her forward, the crowd murmuring as they followed.

"Watch your step," said the man leading her, more a threat than a warning. It didn't do any good anyway.

Cher's ankle struck the edge of what she guessed was a wooden stair. She fell forward, banging both knees against the step above it.

With an impatient sigh, the man hoisted her back to her feet and shoved her up the steps onto a rough platform.

Silence fell. In the distance the gates thudded shut. Only then did the guards remove the sack from Cher's head.

It was early evening, the sun just starting to set. She looked down from a hastily-built stage into the eyes of her audience. None of them, not one, would look her in the eye. Whenever her gaze met theirs, they hastily turned away, staring down at their feet or up into the sky.

Maybe some of them were ashamed. Embarrassed by their own thirst for blood. But she suspected most of them were just afraid of her. No doubt the Winstons had been cooking up all kinds of ludicrous lies about her.

The only ones who did not look away were the ghosts sprinkled here and there throughout the oblivious crowd. All the original judges and all the accusers, eager to see their horrible traditions carried on.

Not a single friendly face in sight.

Behind her, she felt a hungry presence. She glanced over her shoulder to see an ancient, blackened tree looming over her. Although it looked as though it had been dead for a century, something alive roiled within it.

From its branches swung several bodies. The second Cher saw their rotting toes, she whipped back around and squeezed her eyes shut to stop the world spinning around her.

"Make way!" came a voice somewhere ahead of her, and she opened her eyes again to see the crowd part for Nora Winston.

Dean was nowhere in sight. Nor was his father, the mastermind behind it all. Dean's absence Cher could understand; even if his mother did buy into the act he'd put on in the cell, his history with her made him a potential weak link, and no doubt Nora wanted this trial to go as smoothly as possible.

But she had expected Bernard to be here, pulling all the strings.

Nora climbed the steps and came to a halt well away from the accused, folding her hands behind her back and smiling at the crowd.

"People of the Court of Oyer and Terminer." She spoke

so softly the onlookers barely dared to breathe. "I'm sure you all recognize this...woman." She sneered in Cher's direction, and a man at the front of the crowd hacked up a glob of saliva he spit onto the stage.

Everyone had a name for Cher they hissed at her: *witch, spawn of Satan, demon, monster, hag.*

"Two nights ago," said Nora, putting on her best news anchor voice, "Charity Olmstead strolled into the town square of Oyer, where we have built a safe, wonderful community for all of you to live in peace. Foaming at the mouth like some rabid beast, she attacked my niece, Ava, as she drew water from the well for a thirsty child. Fortunately, Ava has trained in self-defense with our brave soldiers. She managed to fight Miss Olmstead off before the witch could shove her into the well. Many of you came to see what the commotion was, and before we could apprehend the threat, she drew some blood, biting and clawing three of our folk."

More hisses and obscenities from the crowd.

But none of this made sense. Nora was lying.

"Your community is walled," Cher said, speaking up without considering the consequences. "How did I get in?"

The guard with the iron poker struck her across the shoulder-blades, sending her stumbling forward with a gasp. She fell to her knees. As she lifted her head, she glimpsed in the audience the ghost who had attacked her back at the house, giving her a teasing wave.

The truth struck her at once. She'd been possessed.

Like a puppeteer, the ghost had taken control of her and delivered her to Danvers. That was why she couldn't remember anything about the journey.

Nora crossed her arms. "Deny the accusations all you

want," she said. "There is evidence. The scratches and teethmarks on our people's skin are proof enough. And we all know what we saw with our own eyes." She turned back to the audience. "Isn't that right?"

The crowd roared.

"Do you have anything to say in your defense before we bring in witnesses?" Nora said, pretending she cared to hear the answer.

No. If Cher admitted the truth, they would still twist it against her. If she had attacked Ava of her own free will—which she hadn't—she was a witch. If she had been possessed by a ghost, she was still a witch, trapped under the influence of evil spirits.

There would be no convincing these people to let her live. Especially not Nora, who was determined to kill the woman who had come so close, *so* close to taking off Dean's rose-colored glasses. Maybe, from the perspective of someone who was so obsessed with power, it had looked like Cher *was* trying to sabotage the Winstons' hold over Salem. But all she had wanted was for Dean to use his privilege for good. She knew he had a conscience, a heart—despite his parents.

What did Charity Olmstead have to say in her own defense?

Nothing except, "He will never forgive you for this." She climbed back to her feet, speaking only loud enough for Nora to hear. This was between the two of them. And Nora knew full well who "he" was.

Nora did not shriek or attack Cher in a fit of rage. She stood perfectly still, eyes narrowed, hands balled into fists at her sides.

She shook her head and repeated what she'd said in the dungeon. "He doesn't love you, you know. He never did."

"You're wrong."

Nora's smile returned. "Just you wait."

And so the seeds of doubt were planted.

Dean claimed he wouldn't let Cher die, but how many times in their years together had he let her down? How many times had he said he was going to resign from the police force, only to let his father guilt him into staying?

No, surely Nora was only bluffing. Dean did love her, Cher knew he did.

But did he love her enough to stop this?

Worse yet—could he have lied to her?

She trusted him so instinctively, so implicitly when he asked her to, trusted the way he abused her in front of his mother and the guards was all an act until he could come up with a plan to break her out.

But what if it was the other way around? What if he was fooling *her*?

Nora straightened her spine and turned back to the crowd. "People of the Court," she said, "as you can see, Mayor Winston is not here right now to preside over the trial. Nor is Ava, who would be a key witness. Both are out on patrols, working hard to protect us from more evil.

"But even without Ava's testimony, we have plenty of evidence to move this trial forward, and—as Deputy Mayor— I believe it is important to rush this case so justice can be served as quickly as possible, and we can be rid of this danger. Since you are all a part of the Court, I ask for your approval."

She asked, and she received. Those gathered in front of the platform clapped.

"Alright then. With that," said Nora, "I call forward our first witness. Little Bethany, please come tell us about the night you saw this woman attack Miss Ava."

* * *

Ferry crept up and down and around the hill where Charity's childhood home stood for hours, craning his neck to peer into the windows every now and then. He saw no sign of anyone inside. He had told her to expect his return before dawn, but she was nowhere to be seen now and the sun would rise soon. Was she asleep?

To make things worse, he had lost her scent when he called off their contract.

In fact, he sensed nothing from her at all. His mind was far too quiet, and it dawned on him Cher's constant link to him—the link of a witch to her familiar, he *finally* admitted to himself—was severed. Not just weakened by distance, but gone entirely.

None of this was right.

Just then a shadow drifted overhead. It was the phoenix, Sunny. He circled once above Ferry then plummeted down, landing with a heavy *thump* in the grass and only barely managing to keep his feet.

"You look worse," Ferry said.

Sunny ignored the jab. "Thank goddess I found you," he breathed. "Evelyn's missing."

"*What?*" Ferry tensed. His first thought was Evelyn had found Cher and done something to her in retribution for stealing her grimoire.

"I went out to hunt some mice and came rushing back when she called for help," Sunny said. "When I got back the whole glade was trashed. They—they killed the troll. She's dead."

"How?"

"Spears. There were four of 'em in her back and one in her throat." His beady eyes were wide with fright, and his feathers lay so flat he looked almost skeletal. "I don't get it. We thought we were safe. Everyone's so afraid of those woods with the dragon sleeping there, we were sure they'd never come looking for us—"

"And Evelyn?"

"No sign of her anywhere. No blood or nothing. I think they took her to Danvers. Look, buddy, I need your help. Please. I know she tried to hurt Charity, but we need to break her out of there. They'll kill her."

"Sunny," said Ferry, "Charity—"

"What's all the racket out here?" A cat leapt onto the porch railing behind them. He licked a paw and sniffed. "You smell like the stranger. Are you her familiar?"

"Stranger?" Ferry said. "You mean Charity?"

"Yeah. She reeked of mildew. Like you."

Ferry flattened his ears. He rather liked the smell of mildew. "Which way did she go?" he asked.

"What's it to you?"

"I'm Ferry, a friend of hers."

Sunny chirped. "She *named* you?"

The cat's ears perked up. "So you *are* her familiar?"

Yes, Ferry thought, but he still could not admit it aloud. "I'm not—"

"Sounds like you are now," said Sunny. "Like it or not."

"Yes." The cat made a sound in its throat that sounded like a snicker. "Once they name you—"

"*Which way did she go?*"

139

Ferry clacked his teeth together and the cat's tail puffed up.

He hissed indignantly and grumbled, "Last I saw, she packed up all her stuff and strolled out the front door like some zombie, right into the rain. There was a man with her, holding her hand. Smelled dead."

For a moment Ferry forgot to breathe. "Was the man a ghost?"

"Yeah, I s'pose. He was all gray and drab and a little transparent." The cat twitched his whiskers. "I understand she and Maya were...close once. So when I saw your witch leave without saying goodbye, I figured something was up. Woke up Maya and Jules right away, and we looked for your friend for hours. But we couldn't find her. I'm sorry. She just vanished."

Sunny glanced at Ferry. "You think they took her to Danvers too?"

"No doubt."

The phoenix kicked off the ground and fluttered in the air. "I'll meet you there," he said, then added slyly, "my fellow familiar."

Before Ferry could bite his tail feathers, he took off at lightning speed.

"Wait!" Ferry called. "You fool, we need a plan!"

Alistair held a paw to his nose, shielding his face from the mud Ferry kicked up as he galloped off.

"You're welcome," he huffed, hopping down from the railing and heading back through the doggy-door into the house.

What an odd pair, he thought to himself. Yet he couldn't shake the feeling the kelpie and the phoenix were some sort of bad omen. The stranger too, that Charity Olmstead. Everything about them screamed *doom*.

No, he did not like any of this at all.

* * *

Eleven. Eleven strangers testified against Charity, sneering and spitting at her until the sun sank and the moon replaced it.

The child, Bethany, claimed to be the only one near the well with Ava Winston when Cher appeared in town, so the story went. She described the attack in a shy, uncertain voice, pausing after most sentences and waiting for Nora to nod. Like an actress unsure of her lines.

"And did you see where the witch came from, sweetheart?" Nora prompted.

Bethany's face went blank for a moment, eyes glazed over. Only Cher saw the ghosts of two little girls standing behind her, whispering ideas black as smoke into her ears and smiling all the while. Bethany herself wasn't aware of their presence, not even as their dark magic jogged her fabricated memory.

"I saw her swoop down from the sky?" she said, more a question than an answer. "And leap off a broomstick? She —she jumped off the broom before attacking Miss Ava. Yeah."

Bethany gnawed at her lower lip and twirled the hem of her skirt in her fingers, until Nora gave her a beaming smile of approval. The child grinned back and stood straighter, more confident.

A lie. It was all a lie, for which she was rewarded with

a pat on her head before Nora sent the girl scurrying back to her parents in the audience.

One by one Nora called up the ten other witnesses, who had allegedly come running when they heard Bethany crying for help. No one else mentioned a broom ride, but they all described the attack in the same way, claiming the witch appeared to have super-human strength. Like a wild animal, she bit and scratched Ava and shoved her closer and closer to the well in the village's center.

According to the last witness, Cher's mistake was putting Ava in a headlock; Ava managed to drop her weight and toss the witch over her shoulder, throwing Cher breathless into the dirt and then knocking her unconscious with the handle of a machete.

When the eleventh witness stepped down from the platform, Nora lifted her chin higher and said, "Now, for our final witness." She folded her hands behind her back. "Tonight, Charity Olmstead stands trial for not one, but two crimes. The first, attacking my niece. The second, bewitching my son. Dean," she called, "you are our last witness tonight. Come."

The crowd parted again, this time craning their necks.

Dean didn't appear.

The crowd grew restless, murmuring among themselves. Nora glared at Cher, and then called even louder, "Dean! It's time."

Everyone watched the gates for a heartbeat, two, three.

Then a whinny broke the night.

"Ferry," Cher breathed.

The gates of Terminer crashed open, and in raced—not

the kelpie—but three men on horseback. Cher's hope wilted.

"What is the meaning of this?" Nora snarled as the soldiers came skidding to a halt before the platform. "Where's Dean?"

"He's back at Oyer, ma'am," one of the men replied. "We've caught her."

"Who?"

"The Grand Witch," said another soldier. "We captured Evelyn Wyse."

Chapter Sixteen

Nora gave a signal and someone slammed the sack back over Charity's head.

Through the burlap, Nora's voice was muffled. "Good news and bad news, everyone. Unfortunately, this trial is on hold for now. But the good news is, we'll likely watch *two* witches hang tomorrow evening, including the very one who orchestrated the end of our world."

The crowd jeered as the guards jerked Cher's chain and led her back off the platform.

"Lock her back up," Nora ordered them. She didn't sound too happy. Not surprising, considering she'd been chomping at the bit to watch Charity die.

The march back to Oyer was more like a brisk jog, with the guards tugging Cher forward and the crowd surging at her back. How quickly the novelty of her trial had worn off, overtaken by excited, hungry whispers about Evelyn Wyse.

The Grand Witch, they'd called her. None the wiser about her lost powers.

When they arrived back at the cell, the guards did not remove the sack from Cher's head right away. She heard rattling chains—not her own—and quiet murmuring across the room.

"Is that Olmstead?" said a woman, and Cher recognized the voice as Ava Winston's.

The two of them had met several times at Winston family dinner parties, when Dean and Cher were still engaged. Ava was just a younger Nora, the daughter she'd never had, proud and constantly sneering. Cher never liked her. The feeling was mutual.

"It is," a guard responded, shoving Cher across the room.

Fingers brushed against her neck and suddenly the zip-tie tightened, just enough to make breathing uncomfortable.

"Good," said Ava, patting her on the cheek through the burlap. "Chain her away from the other one so they can't help each other escape. Hurry. We have a celebration to prepare."

Her footsteps faded out the door.

Someone pushed Cher down onto the lumpy mattress. Cold iron closed around her ankles again, and then the guards yanked the sack off her head.

There was a brief moment where she glimpsed Evelyn, slumped and unconscious, chained against the far wall, wearing the same type of plain shift she herself wore, her white hair wet and combed. They had cleaned her up, just like they had Cher, to give the illusion of civilization.

But they didn't give the old woman the courtesy of a bed, instead leaving her lying on the dirt floor.

She looked so different, so small and frail, when she wasn't buried in layers of robes and chunky jewelry. Her dozen crystal necklaces were gone, replaced by a plastic zip-tie because the Court of Oyer and Terminer had no idea Evelyn Wyse was a witch without her magic.

The witch hunters took their candles and left their victims in the dark. The door slammed shut.

Cher had thought she would be more afraid to be alone with Evelyn again, after the incident in her cave. But she only felt sorry for the old witch.

"Evelyn?" she said. Her voice cracked with disuse. She'd been so quiet throughout the trial, silently letting the judgment roll over her and stamp out the little hope she'd grown over the last couple of days with Ferry. If she had any care left to give, she might hate herself for letting the emptiness consume her again.

"Evelyn," she repeated, tugging her chains in the hope she might be able to cross the room and shake Evelyn awake. But the guards had followed Ava's orders. Cher's chains let her go no further than a foot from the bed. "Evie," she said. "Are you awake?"

"Charity Olmstead."

Evelyn's voice sounded distorted through the dark. Otherworldly, like she was a ghost or possessed by one.

For a second Cher feared just that, wondering if the old Salem spirits had steered Evelyn to Danvers the same way they'd done to her.

The old woman coughed and laughed a single joyless laugh.

"Charity Olmstead," she said again, her voice sounding

more human now, though still raspy. "I once hoped to be your godmother. Will you let me tell you a creation story now? Let it be the one wisdom I pass on to you."

"O-okay," said Cher, unsure how else to answer. She perched on the edge of the mattress.

A long silence followed, and she wondered if maybe Evelyn had slipped back into unconsciousness. But then the old woman took a deep breath and told her story in a strong, almost rhythmic tone:

"Humankind," she said, "is ruled by two sibling gods. The Universe gifted them the Earth as their sandbox, a place to play and create. Together they breathed life into the planet. Together they made the ocean and the sky and the mountains and the deserts. They molded animals to live in these places, plants to grow.

"But one of the siblings wanted a plaything all to himself. So he created human beings.

"For a few hundred years he kept these humans secret from his sister, hiding them in a small corner of the world. He watched them as a child watches ants, while they built and survived and thrived together.

"But soon he grew bored. The whole thing—the whole planet—no longer amused him; he'd outgrown his toys. And so he decided to destroy it all.

"He made himself known to the humans and blessed them—or cursed them—with his own essence. They built temples in his honor and named him Greed. Greed watched with great pleasure as envy seized every human being's heart and turned them against one another. Turned them against the land. The animals.

"Greed's secret could be kept no longer, for the humans' lust for power went well beyond their tiny corner of the world. It was not enough for them. Soon they spread across all of the Earth, tearing down beautiful forests, polluting the seas, wiping whole species off the planet, sucking their dear home-world dry of all it had to give and decimating everything the sibling gods had worked so hard to build together.

"The humans turned on one another too. They enslaved each other, raped each other, killed each other, all to satiate their need for power. All in the name of Greed.

"When Greed's sibling discovered what he had done, she begged him to take it back, to destroy the horrible monsters crawling the Earth. For, as humankind's creator, only Greed could unmake them.

"'No,' Greed replied. 'I quite like being worshiped.'

"His sibling almost gave way to despair. She had poured her heart and soul into creating this world with her beloved brother, only to be betrayed. And there was nothing to be done about it.

"But the sister was cunning, and Greed's words occupied her every waking moment: *I quite like being worshiped.* Such a strange notion it was, worship.

"And then an idea struck: perhaps two could play this game.

"The rules of the Universe said that what one god created, another could not destroy. But there was no rule that said Greed's sister could not create a human being of her own.

"When that human took their first breath, Greed's sibling said to them, 'Go. Go out and fight for this world. For your fellow humans. For me.'

'I will,' the person vowed. 'I will save this planet for you, Love.'

"So the second god was named..."

Evelyn stopped to cough again.

"...And the war was begun," she said eventually, her voice as weary as if she had been there herself when it all started. "That first human Love created died a martyr at the hands of a ruthless emperor, one of Greed's creations. But that person's death stirred something quiet in the hearts of others. Soon resistance against Greed's power spread, even among his own worshipers.

"This war has been going on for millennia. And, although sometimes it seems as though Greed might finally win, Love's magic never fades. It finds a way to live on in her warriors' hearts, and we continue to fight the good fight to restore Earth to its former peace, to make the world as it should be." Another, weaker cough. "Or so the old tales say."

The last notes of the story lingered in the air between teller and listener.

Cher didn't know what to say. She thought the story was meant to be inspiring, but Evelyn only sounded exhausted, defeated as she told it.

After a long pause, the old witch laughed under her breath.

"I want to apologize, Charity," she said. "For what I did to you back in the caves. Or what I tried to do, in my desperation. Blood just has so many magical properties. It's powerful stuff. Just a drop can strengthen any potion, any spell. *More* than a drop, well—I thought...never mind. There is no excuse. I'm sorry."

"I get it," Cher said. "We're all torn between Greed and Love. That's the moral of your story, isn't it? That power corrupts us, even those of us with good intentions. You wanted to stop—this," she gestured vaguely around herself, "even if it meant you had to do something, uh...ethically ambiguous."

"No," Evelyn sighed. "That isn't the moral of the story at all. Let me finish."

"Oh."

Another pause. Then, "Do you know why Bernard Winston wants me dead?" Evelyn asked. "Well, besides the fact I'm a witch, obviously—the One Witch to Rule Them All, if you ask him. But do you know why he *specifically* hunted for me this whole time?"

"No. Why?"

"Last year," she said, "I planned to campaign against him."

"You—? But he's been uncontested for nearly a decade." Surely Cher would have heard if someone finally wanted to challenge Bernard Winston.

"That isn't true," Evelyn said. "Not one bit. Plenty have tried running against him. A few Libertarians he paid off with a chunk of change. Some Democrats who didn't stand a chance. One or two hopeful young Republicans, thinking they might steal the spotlight and the power for themselves, completely unaware of just how tight his hold is on this damned city.

"And then there were the rest of them—the ones like me. The ones hoping to run a grassroots campaign. One for the people. Do you know what happens to those opponents?"

Cher said nothing, only waited for the answer with the heavy weight of dread in her gut.

"We're disappeared," said Evelyn. "Whisked off to prison. Or worse."

"What?"

"Think. How many times in the last few years have you read articles claiming the Salem Police Department, under the guidance of Mayor Winston and his son, the Chief of Police, made some great big drug bust? No culprits named, just an article promising they're working to make Salem a safer city. How often?"

At least once a year. Cher did not say the answer aloud, but Evelyn rightly understood her silence as overwhelming realization.

"Exactly," said the old woman. "I was in a jail cell when the world ended, only a little comfier than this one." She rapped her knuckles against the wall at her back. "They framed me. Planted all kinds of drugs in my shop, then raided it and dragged me off in handcuffs. But when the apocalypse came, breaking those walls down, I escaped."

"Dean..." A whole new wave of righteous, disorienting fury washed over Cher. She had a hard time imagining he knew the truth. Maybe Bernard had sent a lower-ranking officer to plant the evidence.

But what if he didn't? What if Dean had done it himself?

The cell felt suddenly much smaller and more oppressive.

"They think you ended the world, Evie," she said. "And I helped somehow. That's what they told everyone here. They're doing it again. They're framing you. Both of us."

We're going to die.

Evelyn scoffed, but it sounded inauthentic, a mask to hide the fact she felt as frightened as Cher.

"Charity..." Evelyn hesitated, as if she were about to make a confession. Her chains rattled, bare feet brushing against the dirt as she stood. "My powers. She took them. As punishment."

"Who?"

"*Love!*" The word was a hiss. "The goddess, Love, she took my powers away from me."

Evelyn began pacing, the same way she had done back in the caves.

"It's all because I lost faith in her," she said. "I was tired, Charity, so, so very tired of fighting. It felt like—like I was one of the last warriors out there on the battlefield, outnumbered six billion to one. And—for a single second—I listened to Greed's call. I surrendered to him, gave him exactly what he wanted all this time. I m-made a wish."

A sob broke her voice.

"I wished—I wished for the world to end. I willed it to happen. And then it did, that very night. Don't you see?" Her voice was suddenly directed straight at Cher, loud and accusatory. "The war is over. *That* is the moral of the story. We lost."

Through the dark crept those unwelcome fingers of despair, wrapping themselves around Cher. She remembered the smooth stones under her toes, in her fingers as she wandered up the Crane River, filling her pockets and accepting defeat.

A flash of anger pierced her heart. Anger at the world, at Evelyn, at the Winstons. At Ferry. If only he had granted her wish that day and given her the peaceful, enchanted death she had wanted, she wouldn't be here right now, fighting a battle already lost.

Yes, *lost*. Evelyn was right. There was no point; it was all for nothing. Cher couldn't even help the damned kelpie get his revenge now, not in this state. She would die a horrible, painful, public death and Ferry would just have to find a new witch to help him. If there were any witches left by the time the Winstons were done with Salem. If there was any *Salem* left.

From across the room came the sound of Evelyn sliding back down the wall to her seat on the floor. Charity thought for a second the old witch wept, but then she realized the tiny chirping sounds she made in her throat were the sounds of a cackle building and building and then finally breaking through her lips.

"The war's over," Evelyn said, breathless with laughter. "It's over. I'm free."

Chapter Seventeen

Charity thought she would be trapped in the cell with Evelyn for at least another twenty-four hours, but barely one had passed before the door burst open and an entire unit of soldiers stormed into the room.

A few of them had functioning flashlights, the shining glare of the lights blinding the prisoners temporarily. There was a split second before they were both blind-folded again when Cher's eyes adjusted and she caught a glimpse of many weapons. An absurd amount—knives, machetes, and even a sword: handmade short-bows and a few clunky crossbows: pistols, shotguns, and assault rifles. She caught a heavy whiff of alcohol too, unable to pinpoint where it came from.

They were *all* drunk.

Then there was only darkness again as someone threw another sack over her head and tugged her up to her feet.

"Back to the gallows, everyone!" came Nora's voice from outside.

As they marched back to Terminer someone played a drum, another a violin, a third a trumpet, and the crowd at their backs clapped along. It was a happy jig, slightly off-key, that made Cher feel sick to her stomach.

She'd grown used to walking blind and took care to place her feet this time, stumbling now and then but managing to keep her balance.

Evelyn was another story; the soldiers stopped often to tug her up off the ground, the same way they had done to Cher earlier. The only difference was Evelyn seemed to get a kick out of the insults the soldiers spat at her. She'd cackle every time.

After the third or fourth laugh, Cher sensed a shift in the mood. The music turned gradually less hearty, the crowd less festive, and the soldiers stopped snapping at Evelyn whenever she fell.

She heard the click as a gun's safety switched off, someone behind her whispering to their companion, "Just in case, y'know? She's freaking me out."

They still had no clue. No clue how helpless and broken Evelyn really was.

When they reached the platform once more, the hoods were lifted off the witches' heads and Cher found herself face-to-face with dozens of guns and bows trained on her and Evelyn. No one held the witches' chains, but there was no need with so many weapons pointed at them.

In front of the soldiers stood the ghosts of Salem, ignoring the barrels of the guns and the tips of the arrows that passed through their otherworldly bodies. Behind the soldiers huddled the living mob, somber and serious now. The scent of alcohol was overwhelming; some adults still sipped at bottles of beer or liquor. One little girl sat on her father's shoulders to see better, and he swayed beneath her as he took another swig of his drink like they were at a football game.

"Charity Olmstead," said a gruff voice, "Evelyn Wyse."

Bernard Winston stepped up onto the platform, dressed in a wrinkled navy-blue suit, his beard neatly trimmed and fingers covered in gold rings.

He was followed closely by his family: Nora, Ava, and Dean too.

Cher couldn't bring herself to look at Dean, though she sensed him trying to catch her eye. The hour she had spent in the cell had been plenty of time for her to think about everything that had happened since he showed up on the doorstep of her apartment, and she'd made up her mind.

He was unreliable.

Even if he was telling her the truth, even if he really did want to save her from his parents, it was too late. He'd waited too long to act. And now here she was, a noose waiting in front of her nose.

"Good people of the Court of Oyer and Terminer," said Bernard, coming to the forefront of the stage, "I'm sorry to interrupt your celebrations. But the sooner we get this process underway, the sooner our world is free of these dangerous witches. There are many—so many—accusations against both of them this process may stretch out over several days. I only ask for your patience. After all, we do pride ourselves on giving the accused fair and thoughtful trials. We do not rush to assign such grave sentences. We do not pass them lightly. We are not monsters."

Yeah, right. There was nothing fair about any of this. It was clear from the way he called Cher and Evelyn *"dangerous witches,"* from the way the nooses were already prepared, he'd already decided their fate. If she had to guess, Bernard only wanted to stretch out the trials so he could torture them just a little longer before he finally killed them both.

She watched the nooses swing in the breeze.

The first time she'd met Mayor Winston, she'd had difficulty matching him to the man he was on the local news. When the camera was trained on him, when he captivated an audience, he was genial and smiling, warm despite his notoriety. He was good at faking it.

But when Dean introduced Cher to him, he didn't play the part for her. He didn't lift a single corner of his lips, only barely shook her hand and offered a curt, "Hello," before rushing off to talk to someone else, someone more important than his son's girlfriend.

She knew he didn't like her, just like the rest of his family. But she never imagined he would kill her.

"Tonight," Bernard continued, "we will begin with an overview of what these two...women...are accused of." He smiled at them both, as if—by not calling them "witches" for once—he'd done them a favor. Then he stepped aside and gestured to his niece. "Ava."

"Charity Olmstead," said Ava, stepping forward. She wore a pinstriped pantsuit and kitten heels. The family was so desperate to cling to all they once had. "I accuse you of trespassing in Oyer and attempting to murder me."

"I'm confused," said Evelyn, raising her hands. "Are you a witness or a judge?"

Ava raised an eyebrow. "Both," she said.

"Doesn't sound like a fair trial to me." Evelyn shrugged.

Ava lurched forward, fingers curling into fists, but Nora threw an arm out across her chest.

"It is not your turn to speak, Ms. Wyse," Nora said, smiling a sickly-sweet smile. "But thank you for your input." She cleared her throat. "Charity Olmstead, I accuse you of sabotaging the building my son and I sheltered in, resulting in that building's collapse."

"You mean the apartment you stole from me?" Cher said, strangely emboldened by Evelyn's nonchalance. "The one your son kicked me out of?"

She glared at Dean, who paled and shook his head ever-so-slightly; a warning—*Don't incriminate yourself.* But what did it matter? She was a dead witch walking.

"*What*—?" Nora's smile vanished and she glanced sideways at Dean.

Too late, Cher realized her mistake.

Dean had never told his mother she was in the apartment when he went scouting ahead.

Shit. Shit, shit, shit. Breaking out in a cold sweat, she risked a glance in Dean's direction and saw his jaw was tight, but he kept a calm, cool expression.

Nora composed herself, carefully replacing her smile. "You are lucky we escaped," she said, apparently choosing to have the argument with her son at another time when the public wasn't watching. "But you still stand accused of second and third counts of attempted murder against us."

She nodded at Dean to speak next, but she kept her eyes, glinting with hungry anticipation, locked on Cher.

"Charity Olmstead," said Dean, his voice measured and controlled. He took a few steps closer to her. Nora tried stopping him, but he dodged her grasping fingers. "You are accused of bewitching me when we met seven years ago, when you allegedly spiked my drink with some wicked potion."

He closed the space between them and kept his back to his family, to the audience.

"Dean," his mother warned, but he ignored her.

His eyes on Cher's were gentle, apologetic. He reached his left hand up to the right side of her head and stroked her hair. Something sharp dug into the side of her skull and as he tangled his fingers in her hair, she gasped and took a step back. He held tight, hurting her.

Bobby pin, he mouthed so only she could see.

Then he tilted her head back. "What no one here knows is you tried to trick me again," he said, loud enough for everyone to hear, "the night I found you at the apartment."

What the hell was he talking about? Cher felt like she had whiplash, trying to keep up with his twists and turns.

His tracks—he's covering his tracks, making up for the mistake I made, she realized.

Her scalp still throbbed where the bobby pin had poked her. He'd given it to her to escape, to break the zip-tie off whenever she had the chance, and now he was protecting them both from detection.

Keep up, Charity, she willed herself. *This is it.*

But she would hang at the end of the trial. When would she have time to break free?

"After inviting me in, you offered me a drink of water," Dean said, "and thought I didn't see you tip the potion into it. When I turned the drink down, you attacked. What you didn't know was I was armed."

He let go of her hair and grabbed her shoulder, pushed down the neckline of her shift to reveal her shoulder.

"Look!" he said, stepping aside. "I shot her here and she

fled. The wound is gone. She must have healed herself with some spell."

Cher spit at his feet to make the act more convincing.

The crowd gasped, Nora loudest of all. She rushed forward, pulling Dean away from Cher.

"You poor thing," she said. "Why didn't you tell me before?"

"She escaped alive," Dean said. "How could I admit that to you? I was so ashamed."

Cher worried he was overselling it, but Nora fawned over him.

Bernard clapped a hand on each of his wife and son's shoulders, guiding them back to the corner of the platform. He gave a fatherly smile, but his eyes did not match it.

He couldn't possibly suspect the truth—could he?

"That covers Miss Olmstead's crimes," he said, taking center stage again. "Now I will tell you all the story of Evelyn."

The old witch heaved a dramatic sigh. Bernard sucked his teeth and clasped his hands tight in front of him, as if resisting the urge to hit her.

"Evelyn Wyse," he said, pacing back and forth along the edge of the platform, the movement almost hypnotic, "was a criminal well before the end of the world. We arrested her over a year ago on drug charges. The shop she owned, Mandrake's Root, was a front for her drug empire.

"What we didn't expect to find," he continued, reaching into his suit jacket, "was this."

He withdrew a book and held it up for the mob to see.

Evelyn's grimoire.

"This is a witch's spellbook," Bernard explained. "Inscribed in the front cover is Ms. Wyse's own name." He flipped through the pages until he reached the last entry, holding the book open to his audience. "And here is a ritual to bring about the apocalypse."

Cher frowned. She hadn't seen such a spell when she browsed the book herself.

But as Bernard turned to face his victims, brandishing the pages in Evelyn's face like an accusation, she saw he was right; the spell was even in Evelyn's scratchy handwriting. She glimpsed the word blood underlined and traced over several times, making it stand out against the rest of the ritual's instructions.

Just a drop can strengthen any potion, any spell...

Was the ritual the one that had changed everything? And if it was, how much blood had Evelyn needed to shed in order to pull it off?

"Evelyn Wyse," Bernard raised his voice, "I accuse you of ending the world as we knew and loved it, and attempting a genocide of the entire human race."

The crowd erupted, threatening to break like a wave over the soldiers' backs and swarm the platform. The only thing stopping them, Cher recognized, was their precious leader standing between them and their targets.

When the noise died down, Evelyn said, "Mayor Winston, why don't you tell them the truth?"

She sounded different, almost younger, unwavering, words clear as bells. Her voice did not shake or crack or hitch like it had while she told Cher the creation tale.

When Bernard didn't dignify her with an answer, Evelyn barreled on, "You took that grimoire from me when you arrested me," she said, "and kept it in your office. I found it when I escaped during the storms and the earthquakes. That page was miss—"

Bernard straightened his spine and cut her off. "You think you can twist this around on me?" he said, guffawing. "I only kept your book to examine it. It's evidence."

"No. I saw the blood," she said. "It was all over the place, all over the floor and the walls, even the ceiling. I may have wished for the world to end, but *you* completed the ritual." Evelyn's chains rattled as she jabbed a finger in Bernard's direction. "Not me."

A hush fell over the area.

"Bernard?" Nora said, her voice small. "What is she talking about?"

Mayor Winston tossed the grimoire onto the platform and withdrew a revolver from a holster under his jacket.

"Enough," he growled.

He brought the ivory handle down hard on Evelyn's head, so hard blood dripped down her temple. Her eyes fluttered. She laughed once, and then slipped into unconsciousness.

"Do not listen to her words," he said to the mob. "They are laced with an evil curse. Don't you feel it? It's all around us."

He waved his empty hand over the crowd, and the ghosts of Salem scattered among the living. Cher heard their whispers, soft at first and then growing to a maddening susurrus like bugs crawling across her skin.

A black cloud gathered overhead, and screams erupted in Cher's mind. She dared not look up, but she knew what it was without seeing it. The Devourer—it was here.

The people of Danvers shuffled nervously, as if they sensed the menacing presence.

She watched the lines in Bernard's forehead disappear as he watched the ghosts work.

Hang on. He's watching *the ghosts.*

Bernard Winston is psychic. He *summoned the ghosts from the original Trials.* He *controls the Devourer.*

Cher stepped forward, catching her foot in her chains. She stumbled, fell to her knees.

"*He's* doing this!" she yelled at the crowd, but none of them paid her any mind. "He's controlling them! Controlling you! Don't listen to him! Bernard Winston is—"

He whipped around and struck the back of her head with the handle of his gun, and she collapsed.

Chapter Eighteen

A dozen faces loomed over Charity when she finally opened her eyes. Hazy, gray faces. The ceiling above them was a swirling black hole.

She blinked and the scene shifted. The faces flooded with color, solidified, and there was a smell—an awful smell of sweat and waste and blood.

"Show me where you found the witch's marks," someone out of sight said.

Then came someone else's voice from across the room —a woman's. "Don't touch her!" A feral growl to hide her fear. "She is only a child. Don't you dare drag her into this mess—"

A sharp slap and the woman went silent.

Hands reached for Cher. She screamed in a voice both her own and not her own, squeezing her eyes shut, bracing for whatever came next.

When she reopened her eyes, the faces and shadows were gone, though the stench remained. Firelight flickered on the ceiling.

Cher's memory was so foggy she hardly remembered where she had been before she'd lost consciousness. She tried moving her wrists and ankles but found them bound in chains much tighter and shorter than those she'd worn earlier. She lay on a hard, smooth, stone surface. She couldn't turn her head; something cold and thick locked her down—a metal bar.

Something sharp dug into the side of her skull, and for a second, she thought the bar was somehow stapled to her head. Panic stirred up bile in her throat—but then she remembered the bobby pin. Whoever had locked her up here hadn't noticed it, tucked into the layers of her hair.

If only she could reach it.

"Cher?" Evelyn's voice sounded faintly nearby. "Charity, it isn't really happening. Don't panic. They're just visions—"

"Quiet." Bernard. He snapped his fingers and Evelyn gasped through gritted teeth.

Someone snickered—several someones—with an echoing, otherworldly timbre. The ghosts.

Footsteps, then Bernard loomed above Cher. Above him the ceiling was that same churning pitch black, as if a storm cloud were there in the room with them. It stirred more violently when he approached her.

At the sight of his face, memories rushed back to Cher: the trial; Evelyn's accusations; the rush of truth.

They knew the Mayor's secret now.

Any hope she'd had of surviving vanished.

She and Ferry had always suspected the ghosts had something to do with all of this. But she'd thought maybe they'd found a way to possess the survivors living in Danvers. She'd never dreamed anyone living was pulling the strings, least of all Bernard. She knew he was corrupt, but this...

As she stared up at him, horrified, the corners of his lips twitched and he suppressed a giddy smile.

He was enjoying this. He was glad she and Evelyn knew the truth. He couldn't wait to exercise his powers over them.

"I take it you don't understand, Charity," he said, "why I've targeted you. Evelyn and I have a history, but you—your only crime was being engaged to Dean."

He reached for something and held it above her face, idly twisting it around in his fingers. A matchbook.

"I could hardly blame you for that," he continued. "The rest of my family may have thought you were a gold-digger, but I could hardly fault you for wanting to improve your situation in life. In fact, I admired your ambition, even if it meant leeching off of my son. And, of course, I knew you and your parents leaned left politically, but that didn't really matter." He cast a wicked smile in Evelyn's direction. "It never mattered how many of you there were. You outnumbered us, but we held all control. There was never any need for me to fear the loss of an election. Not with President Bates in my corner."

He tucked the matchbook into his breast pocket and strolled to the end of the table. She heard him pick something else up and stack it near her bare feet, but she could not see what it was.

"You never mattered to me," he said. "Even when Dean started dragging his feet like some stubborn ass because of all the doubt you had planted in his brain, I knew I could undo all the damage you did. Coax him back into the fold where he belonged. You were no threat to me."

He paused, pulled the matchbook back out, ripped a match from the bunch.

"Not until I saw your name in dear Evie's grimoire."

Cher frowned. When Bernard noticed this, his smile widened.

"Ah. You had no idea, did you?" He set the match down and pulled the grimoire from inside his jacket. "Here."

He flipped to the page she had never seen—the one with the apocalyptic ritual—and showed it to her. She realized it had been taped back into the book. He must have ripped it out to use it himself, and then put it back in to frame Evelyn during the trial.

"See there?" he said. "'*Need more power. Blood, preferably from other witches. See 'Blood-Letting Rituals,' page 72.*' And here—" He flipped to that page number, the one Cher had skipped over because the memory of Evelyn hovering over her with her knife was too much for her. "Look. '*Charity Olmstead,*' in the margins there with a whole list of other witches' names, all crossed out. Only yours is circled. That certainly piqued my interest, seeing my son's ex-fiancée's name in this book."

He snapped the cover shut and tucked it away again.

Cher tried and failed to shake her head. Something didn't add up.

"But—you had her grimoire *before* the end of the world," she said. "She didn't need my blood until she lost her powers, after the world ended. Unless..."

Bernard lifted his bushy brows. "What's this now?"

He glanced back and held a hand up, a signal to the ghosts. Whatever they were doing to Evelyn, whatever horrible visions of the past they were forcing upon her, they stopped instantly.

"Evelyn has no power left?" Bernard threw his head back and laughed. After a moment he wiped tears from his eyes. "Oh, that's wonderful news. I had no idea. Evie, why didn't you tell me? Too ashamed?"

Evelyn's quiet sobs cut short. She lashed against her bonds with futile fury.

He ignored her and turned back to Cher. "Your name was in this grimoire well before then," he said. "When we raided her shop, we didn't find drugs. We found needles and blood. Hundreds of packs of blood stored in a refrigerator in the basement."

"What?"

"Charity," Evelyn said, "I can explain—"

"Isn't it obvious?" said Bernard. "She intended to use your blood to end the world."

"Charity, darling," said Evelyn, her tone desperate, "you must understand how powerful your blood is. Your parents were some of the most skillful psychics in Salem, much stronger than me. Even if you never wanted to be a witch, all that power in your veins would have gone untapped. If you weren't going to use it..."

She stopped there, perhaps realizing just how deranged she sounded.

Cher's nails dug into her palms as she thought of all the other names on the list, the ones crossed out.

"How many of your friends did you kill?" she asked Evelyn. She couldn't bear to look at Bernard as she spoke— he could hardly contain his delight, pitting his victims against each other.

"I didn't kill them," said Evelyn. "I promise you. I didn't even hurt them. I-I invited friends to visit for some tea, one by one. And when they—when they finished their drinks, they fell asleep—"

"You drugged them."

"It was harmless. I just poked them with a needle, took enough blood to store in a packet. I didn't kill them—"

"You planned to end the world!" Cher's voice ricocheted as if the shadow on the ceiling—the Devourer—threw it back down at her. "That wasn't harmless, Evelyn!"

"I know." She sobbed. "I know. I'm sorry, Charity. It's no excuse, but I'll say it again, the fight is enough to drive anyone mad. I wasn't thinking straight. No one I knew was happy. No one. Not just here in America, but *anywhere*. There was nowhere left to run. It broke my heart."

"You were upset with the world, so you had to ruin it for everyone? You just took it upon yourself to put us all out of our misery?"

"No. No!" She sniffled. "That was not my intention. Like a fool, I thought if I used enough blood, I could maybe hone the ritual and target only specific people. People with ill will. People—people controlled by Greed. I didn't want to end the *whole* world. I just wanted to weed the evil from it once and for all. Of course, it fell right into the hands of one of those people." Her voice softened under the burden of her guilt. "And now we're here. I didn't mean to end the world. Yet here we are. It's all my fault."

Cher didn't know what to say. *I'm sorry* didn't feel genuine enough; she had nothing to apologize for, and she felt far too much disgust and betrayal yet to sort through it all to the pity underneath. *It's alright* was a flat-out lie because none of this was okay.

But she didn't need to reply; Bernard stepped in then.

"So," he said, once more approaching the foot of the

table. "When I saw your name in the book, Miss Olmstead, it jogged something in my memory. Something about your parents. When you were with Dean, I dismissed their little psychic business as a gimmick. A scam.

"But, you know." He sucked at his teeth thoughtfully. "I always saw ghosts myself. The ghosts of my enemies. People I had to...take care of...to get where I was. I just assumed it came with the job. I never suspected they were really ghosts. Just the last vestiges of my conscience playing tricks on me.

"My opinions changed when I found Evelyn's grimoire and decided to play around with some of the rituals in there.

"I drew a few summoning circles in my office and welcomed any spirit to step forward. Imagine my surprise when Samuel Parris himself appeared."

A familiar hiss of laughter sounded across the room. She recognized it as the laughter of the ghost who had possessed her—apparently the ghost of Samuel Parris, a name she knew from her Salem history. He was one of the instigators of the original witch trials.

"We struck a bargain," said Bernard. "I knew I would never truly have to fear losing my seat as Mayor, but I was tired. So, so tired of hunting down those who opposed me.

"Parris offered to help. Together, with all the blood Evie had collected—so helpful of you, Evie—Parris and I summoned the storms and the earthquakes. Those who were loyal to me, I protected. The rest were left to suffer. And if any of them survived, Parris promised to help me lead another witch hunt until the last of you were taken care of."

He sucked in a breath between his teeth.

"What I didn't expect," he continued, "was the dragons and the kelpies, or any of the other monsters. According to the ritual, the world would be shaped into what I wanted. I never asked for dragons."

Evelyn snorted. "*I* did," she said. "You should have cut my throat and thrown my blood into the mix."

Bernard *tsked*. "I guess I should have," he said. "But I thought you would perish with the rest of them in the storms. How naïve of me. Tell me, Evelyn, how did you do it? How did you interfere?"

When she finally answered, after a long pause, Evelyn's voice was thick with tears. "I gave up," was all she said.

"I see," said Bernard, though it sounded like he didn't see at all.

Cher understood though; it was all in the timing. The same moment Bernard finished his powerful ritual, Evelyn made her last wish.

Their willpowers must have clashed. His greed, her love, wrestling for control until the world turned into...this beautiful, horrible mess.

"Anyway, it isn't that important," said Bernard. "Since the world ended, I've been dabbling in other spells, other types of magic. When I failed to find Evelyn's body among the wreckage of the prison, I attempted to scry for her. That showed me nothing. The water's surface remained blank when I asked it to show me where she was.

"I doubted she was dead, though. So, I kept looking. And I looked for every other name on this list—including yours, Charity—in the hopes I might find you and bleed you for all the magic you were worth. That's when I saw you in your apartment."

Cher's heart sank. "So, *you* sent Dean and Nora out looking for me," she said. "To kill me."

"Mm. Tell me the truth," he said. "Did Dean actually shoot you? Or did he let you go? And I'm warning you, Charity Olmstead, you'd better tell me the truth. If you don't.... Well." He tilted his head up to the ceiling. "Show her what will happen to her."

The Devourer twisted and stretched, and all Cher could do was watch it reach for her.

There was a flash of bright light and suddenly she sat in the back of a wagon. Her wrists were thin and bony, a child's wrists, and they were bound with rope.

Salem, 1692. The Devourer was forcing Cher to relive the town's dark history.

A woman in an apron and a bonnet had her arm around Cher, not a protective gesture but a threatening one. With her other hand, the woman grabbed her under the chin and forced her to look at the tree in front of them —and the body jerking as it swung from a rope in the branches.

"Your mommy was a bad, bad person, Dorothy," the woman said, leaning down to whisper in her ear. "Best be careful you don't end up like her."

Hot tears sprang up in Cher's eyes. She blinked, and for a second her perspective shifted. She was the body in the tree, staring down at her own dirty, purpling feet. She had to break the rope. She couldn't breathe, she couldn't breathe—

Just as suddenly the vision vanished and Cher returned to herself, watching the Devourer recede.

"Dean shot me," she croaked. A lie. But she hoped the

very real tears flooding from her own eyes now were convincing enough.

"With what kind of gun?" said Bernard.

Fuck. "I don't know," she said, thinking fast. "I didn't see. I just felt the bullet and ran."

"But he said he shot you in the front of your shoulder. Surely, even if you only glimpsed the gun for a second, you could tell the difference between a revolver and, say, a shotgun."

"It was dark. And it happened so fast. It could have been his pistol. Or a revolver. I don't know."

Bernard sighed. "I think you're lying to me," he said. There came the scratch and sizzle of a freshly-lit match. "I hoped my friends would be able to convince you to confess, but it looks like I'll have to do the work myself."

A snapping, crackling sound, soft at first, then louder. Cher's feet warmed.

And then something hot lashed at the sole of her left foot.

She shrieked and tried to yank the foot back, forgetting it was shackled. Another flame licked at the same foot, then another and another. Her sight blurred with the searing pain and shock. She screamed in agony—so loud she couldn't hear Evelyn yelling her name.

"You know, Cher," said Bernard, sticking his face right up in hers so she could hear him, "my good friend, Samuel Parris, told me where he found you. In some house on the northeastern coast, right on the water. Laying low with some other witchy friends of yours.... Just tell me what I want to hear, and I'll call off my search teams."

No.

"So, I'll ask you one more time. Did Dean let you go?"

Cher shook her head. The bobby pin pressed into her head, a sharp reminder Dean was on her side. He had done so much wrong. But he was in her corner. He had given her hope again. She wouldn't sell him out. She couldn't. There must be a way to protect them all....

Bernard said something else to her, but all she could hear now was the crackling of the flames beneath her feet. Tears soaked her cheeks.

She couldn't keep the darkness at bay. Her vision went black and she slipped away.

* * *

Cher awoke again back in her original cell, lying flat on the lumpy bed. Thinking for half a second the torture had been a nightmare, she sat up—and gasped as she brushed the sole of her left foot across the mattress.

Careful not to let it brush anything else, she crossed her left leg over her right knee and gently touched the tender skin of her injured foot. The burn could have been worse, but it hurt like hell. She barely pressed her finger to the smooth, shiny skin before groaning and yanking her hand away again.

"How are you feeling?" Evelyn's exhausted voice found her through the dark.

Cher didn't answer right away. Instead, she reached up into her hair and pulled out the bobby pin.

"Better than I've felt since we got here," she said, unfolding the pin and feeling for the lock of the zip-tie around her neck.

"Well, at least you've held onto your sense of humor."

"I'm not being sarcastic." She gasped again, cursing

under her breath as she fumbled the bobby pin and nearly dropped it. But she caught it before it fell and exhaled, reminding herself to stay calm. For Dean. For Maya and Juliet. "Do you know any healing spells? I can't walk on this foot."

"Yes, plenty. But I have no powers. Remember? And even if you wanted to try yourself, you've got the zip-tie."

"You mean this?"

Cher tossed the zip-tie across the room in the direction of Evelyn's voice. Then she shut out the fear and the pain and focused on that tiny well of willpower in her gut— until she summoned a blue-hot flame into each of her palms, illuminating the cell with a cool glow.

The fire didn't hurt her. Just like Maya had promised, now Cher had a calm control over her powers, the magic came naturally. She understood it as a part of her.

Evelyn stared in awe as Cher held the magical fireballs up one at a time to the chains between her wrists, then— when those melted—to the ones between her ankles. She still wore the shackles, but they no longer immobilized her.

"How—?" said Evelyn. Then, "The son. Dean. He *did* help, didn't he?"

Cher nodded and hopped on one foot across the room, bobby pin in hand.

"What are you doing?" said Evelyn, as the younger witch started working at the zip-tie around the elder's neck. "Don't waste your time. I have no powers anyway."

Cher chucked the second zip-tie away, then snapped the bobby pin in half. She handed one half to a baffled Evelyn, then took her own half and cut the broken, jagged end into her thumb until a drop of blood welled up.

"Open wide," she said, jabbing her thumb into Evelyn's

mouth. "You're going to heal me. Consider it an apology for getting me into this mess. Hurry up. You too."

Impatient, she grabbed Evelyn's wrist and pricked her wrinkled thumb.

"I could just walk you through the spell," said Evelyn, breathless. "You—you trust me to do this?"

"Not really," Cher admitted. "But it's faster than teaching me how to heal myself. Besides, I don't want Winston to have the satisfaction of killing either of us."

She squeezed a few drops of Evelyn's blood onto her tongue, completing the ritual exchange.

Evelyn's chest heaved. She pressed a hand against her collarbone, reveling in the heat of the magic flooding her core.

Then, without another moment of hesitation, she took Cher's left ankle in one hand and, with the other, traced a rune on the sole of her foot.

It tickled a little, but it didn't hurt. The symbol glowed blue for a moment, and then it faded into the burned skin.

"There," said Evelyn. "Test it out."

Cher did so, pressing both feet firmly into the ground as she stood up.

"No pain at all," she said.

"Then how's about you get me out of these chains and we make our great escape?"

* * *

"You know any unlocking spells?" Cher asked, gesturing to the only exit.

"I do," said Evelyn. They both crouched in front of the door.

But before she could get to work, the door clicked open and swung at them, sending the two witches scrambling backwards.

In stepped a young girl. She couldn't have been more than fifteen.

When she saw the flames in Cher's hands, she dropped the tray of broth she carried, sending the warm liquid spilling everywhere.

"Don't!" Cher said, the magic flames sparking in warning as the girl opened her mouth.

She was smart enough to stifle the scream in her throat —not that Cher would have actually hurt the poor girl. She was only a child.

"What's going on?" came a man's voice, and a guard appeared in the doorway.

Cher aimed the fire at him and sent it hurtling across the room. His sleeve caught instantly.

So much for sneaking out.

She grabbed Evelyn by the wrist, and they shoved the guard aside, dashing out into the hallway.

Just outside they came face-to-face with Dean.

He looked like he'd seen better days. His right eye was swollen and bruised, and there was a cut across the bridge of his nose. But he was armed with a pistol and a machete, and he wore a bulletproof vest.

"I was just about to break you out," he breathed. "Looks like you got it handled. Here." He shoved something into Cher's arms—a book. The grimoire. "Good news is, I got that back for you. Bad news is, we've gotta go. Now. My father's onto us."

"You don't say."

"Come on. Stay close."

"Dean, how are we going to do this? The village walls—"

"The walls are only thin planks of wood," he said. "The second I heard they caught you, I loosened some of the nails in one of them so we can lift it up and slip through. It's just outside. Let's g—"

From outside came rapid gunfire and the loud, piercing caw of a bird.

"Sunny?" Evelyn pushed past Dean and Cher and climbed the ramp. "Sunny!"

"Evelyn, don't!" Cher chased after her, Dean close behind.

There was nothing either of them could have done to stop it.

They arrived just in time to see the reunion—Sunny spotting Evelyn as she waved her arms in the moonlight to greet him. The happy, trilling note he let out, interrupted by one of the soldiers shouting as they caught sight of the old witch. The phoenix's dive, his tail-feathers trailing the ground and striking the dirt like a match, creating a wall of flames to hide Evelyn from the soldiers' view.

The tiny bullet piercing the bird's chest.

He bounced once, twice, and skidded to a halt at Evelyn's feet.

A banshee's wail. Evelyn fell to her knees, lifting her familiar into her arms and tracing healing runes above his heart over and over and over again.

Dean tugged at Cher's sleeve, but she could only watch Evelyn and Sunny, stunned and helpless. When she didn't move, Dean hurried over to Evelyn's side and tried to help the old woman to her feet.

"*Leave me alone!*" She swiped at Dean, bloody fingers clawing the air.

Tucking Sunny under one arm, she staggered to her feet and moved towards the wall of flames. In their light she looked wild, her hair plastered to her sweaty forehead, eyes reflecting the fire.

She turned back and looked at Cher, a smile softening her face for just a second.

"Thank you," the old witch said. "You keep going now, alright? Don't let these bastards take Salem from us."

"*Evelyn!*" Cher shouted, but she was too late. The witch stepped through the wall of phoenix flames, magically unharmed.

All Cher could hear on the other side of the fire were shouts and screams and gunfire.

She wheeled around when she heard a sharp crack behind her. A plank of the fence went flying, then another, and another, until there was a hole wide enough for the creature on the outside to fit through.

She saw the glowing esca first.

"*Ferry!*"

She ran to him and threw her arms around his bony neck. Already she felt the weight of the last few days dissipate, all the mental and physical scars healing because he was back. Ferry was back.

"Cher, get away from that thing!"

It was Dean who called to her. Dean who pointed his gun at the kelpie, *her* kelpie, and flicked the safety off.

She turned her back to Ferry and faced Dean.

"Don't be ridiculous," she said. "He's my familiar."

Ferry did not deny it.

Smiling, she swung up into the kelpie's saddle. Dean lowered his weapon, jaw agape.

"Hurry," she said to him. "Let's get out of here."

"Cher..." said Ferry, uncertain.

"It's okay," she said. "Dean's on my side."

He approached Ferry like a mouse sniffing out a trap. Cher held a hand out to him.

"Come on," she said. "Up-up."

Ferry tensed the second Dean touched him. "Where is Sunny?" he asked, trying to ignore his discomfort. "And Evelyn? Sunny and I hurried here together once we realized you'd both been taken. We've been just outside the walls, coming up with a plan. But we were separated when one of the guards patrolling the walls spotted us and fired."

Cher's relief faltered. In her happiness at finding Ferry again, she'd already forgotten about Evelyn. Like it was all some bad dream she didn't have to worry about.

"They..."

She shut her eyes against fresh tears, fighting back the memory.

Ferry watched it all in her mind's eye, everything she and Evelyn had been through during the trials, in the dungeon, how close they had come to escaping together just seconds ago—and Sunny's fate.

"I see," he said with a twinge of grief. If the phoenix was mortally wounded, he wouldn't be reborn. "Damn."

"We could wait for them," Cher said.

Dean, sitting behind her in the saddle, didn't interrupt; he seemed to understand she was talking to the kelpie, though he couldn't hear the creature's words.

"We're sort of safe here, right? No one's getting past that wall of fire. Evelyn might still be alive. She might have healed Sunny." She clung desperately to that hope. There was still gunfire, still shrieks of pain and fear. Evelyn was still fighting. She had to be. "Let's wait."

"Cher, we need to go," said Ferry gently. "It's too risky. That batty old witch has made up her mind."

He tried and failed to inject a little venom into his tone, for he still harbored some resentment towards Evelyn after the stunt she had pulled back in the forest.

Yet he was grateful to her too, for all she had just sacrificed to help Cher escape.

How his heart ached for her. For Sunny. What if that had been him, leaping to defend Cher?

"Right." Her voice cracked. "Yeah. You're right. Bernard knows where Maya and Juliet are. We can't wait." She swallowed a lump in her throat. "Let's go."

Dean squeezed his arms around her waist. "I'm sorry," he said.

She leaned back against his chest as Ferry turned them around and stepped through the gap in the broken fence, taking them far, far away from that nightmare.

Chapter Nineteen

Ferry found them a shallow stretch of the Crane River and crossed there. After they galloped south for a short while and came to a halt, Cher realized she recognized this stretch of bank.

He'd brought her right back to where it all began.

Dean slipped off the kelpie's back, mumbling something about needing to stretch his legs, and wandered off into the copse of trees nearby. Once Cher dismounted, Ferry trod back into the river, whinnying softly at the familiar water's cool, refreshing embrace.

Cher sat at the water's edge and splashed the dirt and sweat and grime from her face. Every tiny sound across the river, every snapping twig or bird call, set her on edge.

"Don't worry," Ferry said. "No one will follow us. I stomped traces of my illusory magic into any hoof-prints I left. If someone tries tracking us, they'll think we're traveling in the opposite direction."

Cher nodded, but she remained quiet. Stubbornly quiet.

"Alright, well, I expected a little admiration for that trick," Ferry said, huffing a breath through his nostrils. "I am sorry. Okay? I am truly, truly sorry we argued and I threw a temper tantrum and left you alone for hours."

She crossed her arms.

"But it isn't my fault you decided to go summoning ghosts unsupervised."

She glared daggers at him. "How do you know—?"

"I ran into a cat who saw the whole thing."

Alistair. What a little tattletale.

"Lucky he did, too," Ferry continued, "or else I would have had no clue where you were. I couldn't sense your presence anywhere, couldn't even pick up your blood-scent."

Cher's indignation caved under a smile. "You *do* care!" she said. "Stop denying it already."

"Yes...I care about the promise you made me," he said, not quite as wholehearted as he had been when he'd denied her accusations in the past. "I am just a monster looking forward to his next meal. Remember?"

"No." Her smile faded. "You're not a monster. Ferry, you..." Her eyes glittered. She laughed uncomfortably and wiped the tears away. "You are the very definition of compassion."

Wading hip-deep into the water, she pressed her forehead between his hideous eyes. His esca tickled the top of her head.

"You have more heart than most human beings I know. And that inspires me to be better. Thank you."

Ferry didn't move. "Cher, what are you saying?"

A couple of tears escaped her control, slipping down her cheeks. "I made a deal with you," she said. "And I stand by it. But you were right, Ferry. I don't want to die—yet. I want to fight first. I will get revenge—for you, for Evelyn and Sunny, for *me*—if it's the last thing I do."

He took a step back. "It was the Winstons, you know," he said cautiously. "They're the ones who led the attack against me and my mate. The mother, Nora, was the one who killed her."

"Oh." She supposed that wasn't so surprising.

"Cher, I...I think they were after *me*," said Ferry. "Specifically me. They didn't attack just because they were afraid of monsters in general. A few days ago, while you were napping in that patch of clover—you remember?"

She nodded.

"I saw a ghost," he explained. "A little girl. One of the ancient ones. I thought she was spying on my spawn. But when she saw me, she said something. She said, 'Did we get the wrong one?'"

His next words were slower, more thoughtful as he reflected on all Cher had told him earlier of Bernard Winston, the man who led the witch hunters. "Winston said he hunted for you after he saw your name in Evelyn's grimoire, yes?"

Cher nodded again.

"I believe," he said, "perhaps his minions—the ghosts— they'd been lurking around Salem for weeks, you know. I saw them all over the place. And I think they some- how...sensed...something in me. A connection to you. And so, perhaps, they warned Winston to keep an eye out for any kelpies."

"A connection? But we hadn't even met yet when the Winstons attacked you."

"No. We hadn't."

The words hung there between them and all at once she understood what he was implying.

A connection. Like the kind between a witch and her familiar.

But Ferry didn't say it. That was fine. She knew.

"So, that is why the Winstons attacked us," he said instead. "They were looking for *me,* for the kelpie who would...who would help you develop your powers. They hoped to weaken you so you would be easier to capture. Bernard and his ghosts were afraid of what would happen if we met."

Cher took a few steps backwards, her expression blank, nose turning red as more tears threatened to spill over. She plopped down on what she thought was the riverbank, only to realize she was still ankle-deep in the water.

"It's my fault then," she said, her eyes finding Ferry and focusing on him. "I'm so sorry. It's my fault they killed her."

"No, Cher, that's not what I'm saying. No. It's Bernard Winston's fault."

She nodded yet again, but she didn't seem convinced.

"And Charity, our contract...I—"

He stopped short as Dean returned. The kelpie's lips had long been chewed away by the river's fish, but his jaw tightened in what could only be described as a snarl.

Cher noticed it, that flash of rage. And when she noticed it, she caught a glimpse of something—a memory? A hand on his saddle. A prick of blood. The shrieking, agonized screams of his mate. A knife in her shoulder. No, in *Ferry's* shoulder. The hard snap of his teeth, his kicking hooves, gasping for breath as he chased Dean and Ava and Nora and their soldiers away, away, until they climbed a steep cliff and just barely escaped his wrath.

And then Cher's own memory—Dean's bandaged hand, the night he appeared at her apartment.

She shook her head, clearing the visions away. How often Ferry read her mind, sifting through her brain like an old photo album. Now they understood the bond between them better, maybe the wall around his mind had transformed into a sieve.

His mind was hers for the reading too.

"Ferry?" she said. "What was that? What did I just see?"

It was Dean, she expected him to reply. *It was Dean who prevented me from saving her life.*

Are you going to kill him? she wanted to ask. She'd unknowingly served Ferry's revenge to him on a silver platter. Or a portion of it, at least.

And if she had to choose between Dean and Ferry, who would it be?

Ferry hesitated. "I'm going to see my spawn," he said. "To check on him. He's just downriver a little ways. I take it you two could use some time alone anyway, yes?"

To say my goodbyes? Cher wondered.

Instead, "Things never go well when we separate," she warned.

"Yes, well, I won't be long, not like last time. I promise. Just be careful, alright?"

He sank underwater before she could reply.

Ferry found his spawn snacking on a frog on the banks of his estuary. The colt hardly spared his sire a glance when he heard his approaching splash.

"You're still alive," the colt said, with only the tiniest hint of surprise in his inflection.

"Don't sound so enthused," Ferry replied, wading to shore. "I'm glad to see you're doing well. Anything new?"

The colt chewed his meal without any rush, answering only after he swallowed the last of the frog and heaved himself back up onto his feet. "I...have been visiting the other kelpie you mentioned," he said, tensing as if he dreaded his sire's reaction.

"I see," said Ferry. "And does that mean you're...?"

"Mates? Not yet."

"But you like him?"

"I enjoy his company."

"Good!" Ferry's jaw stretched into what might be interpreted as a grin. He closed the gap between himself and his spawn and nuzzled his nose against the colt's. "I'm happy for you."

"Where's the meal you promised me?"

"Ah. Enough of the small talk then. Just want to cut right to the chase, don't you?"

The colt didn't answer.

"She's upriver," Ferry said.

"So you haven't exacted your revenge yet." A statement, not a question.

"Correct." A pause. Should he tell him?

Yes. Yes, of course. His colt deserved the truth.

"Come," he said. "Let's swim a bit. I'll tell you everything I know."

Ferry dipped back into the water. The colt joined him eventually, though he dragged his hooves the whole way to the water's edge.

Once he joined his sire, they both relaxed. It was nice

to swim together like this, like the old times, before the magic called them out of hiding, when the colt barely had his bearings yet and his fins were too big for his scrawny ankles. Ferry missed those afternoons. Kelpies grew up far, far too quickly.

Once they were settled, Ferry recounted what he'd seen in Cher's memories. He explained how the ghosts were working with the humans who attacked them, a family called the Winstons. He explained they'd all been after him. That his mate was only caught in the crossfire, and her death was excessive, just the cost of some ugly human war that never ended. And she wasn't the only one to die needlessly. Sunny was gone now too, who'd been like family to the kelpies for so long; and his witch Evelyn, who certainly wasn't perfect, but who deserved a far better ending than the one she received.

"I don't follow," said the colt. "Why were these humans after you?"

Ferry took a deep breath. He locked his eyes on the colt's. "Because somehow they knew the truth: I am Charity Olmstead's familiar."

He expected backlash, just like the last time they'd talked.

But to Ferry's surprise, the colt simply reached out with his mind and brushed against his sire's memories.

He watched their entire story unfold in his mind's eye.

His sire met this Charity Olmstead less than a week ago, and yet, as he learned of all they had been through together, the colt's heart warmed.

For the first time since his dam died, his sire's thoughts seemed brighter, more colorful.

The colt did not fully understand why his sire's fate

intertwined with the witch's. But it was clear they were destined to meet all along.

"Okay," was all he said. No fight. Just acceptance or, at the very least, tolerance.

Ferry breathed a sigh of relief.

"Once the Winstons are dead and the ghosts are exorcised," he finished, "or—if Charity and I don't survive..." He gave a gruff snort and shook water from his mane, banishing the thought. "Whenever one side or the other wins, you will be safe. Please, please promise me you will lay low until this is over. Stay underwater as much as you can. No more laying about on shore and enjoying the sunrise. The ghosts must have told Bernard by now he got the wrong kelpie, so they'll probably keep hunting our kind until they get the right one. I'll let you know when it's all over."

"If you can," said the colt.

"If I can."

"And if I don't hear from you, should I just assume...?"

"That I'm dead. Yes. Give it a couple of weeks. But I truly don't think it will be much longer. Things are sort of coming to a head." He paused. "I already told you Charity is upriver. She's...with one of the Winstons right now," Ferry admitted.

The colt's mouth watered so dramatically a glob of saliva dropped from it. He lifted his head higher, ear-stubs perked up. "You're joking?"

Ferry shook his head.

"Well, I wish you'd gotten here sooner then! If I'd known I was about to get a full meal, I wouldn't have had that snack."

"It isn't that simple," said Ferry. "This one, he—he

turned his back against the rest of the family. He helped Cher escape."

The colt's teeth clamped together tightly. "So you're going to spare him?"

Of course not, Ferry thought. His blood still boiled at the thought of Dean getting in his way. If Dean hadn't been there during the attack, Ferry might have saved his mate. He resented Nora Winston for delivering the killing blow, but he hated Dean just as much—perhaps even more —for interfering.

Revenge was so close, he was frankly shocked he'd managed to hold himself back for this long.

But what would it cost me, to kill him?

For some reason far beyond the kelpie's comprehension, Cher loved Dean. If he died, she'd be devastated.

If Ferry killed him, she might never forgive him.

Yet his own colt might never forgive him if he let Dean walk free.

"We'll see," he said finally. "Please—let's just swim together a little longer. Could I meet your new friend?"

The colt sighed. "Fine. Yeah. Let's go."

"Good."

Ferry didn't know what lay ahead. He wanted to be sure if he couldn't be here to take care of his spawn, at least he'd be leaving him in good hooves.

* * *

Dean pulled a granola bar from one of the pockets of his bulletproof vest and handed it to Cher. She took it from him but didn't open it.

"Not hungry?" he asked.

190

"Starving, actually," she said. "It just might be another day before my appetite comes back." She handed the granola bar back to him. "Y'know, I don't have any pockets. Why don't you hold onto this for me?"

He took it and pulled something else out from inside one of his pockets: a ring of keys.

"Here," he said, taking one of her hands. She still had all four shackles clamped around her wrists and ankles; the chain itself had been much thinner, much easier to melt with her fire-spell.

When Dean unlocked the last shackle with a crudely-made iron key, he said, "I'm sorry I didn't have time to grab the rest of your belongings. You must be chilly."

Cher shrugged. "At least we're out of there."

"Yeah."

She didn't know what she had expected. Wasn't this what they'd both yearned for, even before the end of the world? To get the hell away from his family and run away together? She wanted to believe this might finally be the beginning of their Happily Ever After.

But her heart ached so much, and there were so many questions. So much he had to answer for, before she knew whether she could trust him.

Now Ferry had left them together, she was afraid to be alone with Dean. Never mind he hardly seemed a threat now, slouching on the shore with his legs splayed out in front of him, picking chocolate chips out of a second granola bar and savoring them.

A granola bar he stole from *her* cupboards, she suddenly realized. They were her favorite, oatmeal and chocolate chip. She bit back her resentment.

"Dean," she said, so softly he almost didn't hear her

over the flow of the river. "Dean, can I ask you some things?"

"Of course," he said around a mouthful of food.

Okay. Where to begin?

"Did you know Evelyn Wyse?"

He frowned at her and swallowed before answering. "I mean—I knew *of* her," he said. "I knew why my father was after her these last couple of months. She was a powerful witch, right? One of the most powerful in Salem."

"I mean before the apocalypse. Did you know her then?"

Did you frame her? she didn't ask.

They both stared at one another, Cher searching for any tells he might be lying, and Dean looking...for what, exactly? Was he trying to gauge what answer she wanted to hear?

"No," he finally told her. "Everything my father said at the trial, all that about the drug bust, it was all news to me."

"Didn't you give the orders?" She couldn't help the edge of anger creeping into her tone. She didn't believe him. How could she? How could he not know? Wasn't he the Chief of Police? Didn't his force keep him up to date on all major cases? Especially one as big as that.

"No," he said.

Apparently deciding this was too serious a conversation for snacking, he folded the granola wrapper back up and tucked the second half into his pocket again.

"Cher, you have to understand. My father was Chief of Police before me, and even though he's been Mayor for a while now, most of the officers still listened to him. He went behind my back sometimes, gave them assignments I didn't find out about until much later. Actually—I'm starting to think he did it a lot more often than I ever knew."

He was so pale in the dim, gray light of dawn. "I swear, I had nothing to do with Evelyn's arrest."

He was saying exactly what Cher had suspected was the truth, back when Evelyn recounted her history with Bernard.

So, why was it so hard for her to believe him?

Oh, Dean, what is this horrible wedge your family drove between us? How do I take it out?

"Okay," she said. "Next question then. You told me you stole the apartment from me to set up an outpost."

Dean broke eye contact and she knew she'd caught him in a lie.

"Your father told me he sent you to kill me," she said. "I don't get why you would have lied to me, especially at that point. I mean, I was captured. I knew what your parents planned to do to me. What was the point?"

Dean dragged his hands down his face. "I don't know," he sighed.

"Why didn't you just say you had sneaked ahead of everyone else to warn me—"

"I don't know!" Dean snapped, and Cher flinched. "I'm —I'm sorry, I didn't mean—Cher, do you know how hard it is to accept your parents are murderers? Even knowing what they had in store for you, after witnessing all the other trials they held...I just couldn't admit it. Not out loud. I was too disgusted. Too ashamed." He paused, glancing ruefully at her. "We *did* want the apartment as an outpost."

"But that wasn't the primary reason you were there."

"No. You're right." Dean crossed his legs. "I'm sorry. I

know a lot doesn't add up. It's been hard, trying to play the double-agent. But we're free of all that now. Please, can you just trust me? Can't we leave all that behind us?"

Maybe someday. But I just don't know.

"One last question," she said instead.

Cher took his hand, the one that had been bandaged when he arrived at her apartment. She flipped it over in her lap, examining the palm.

There was a scar in the shape of a perfect dotted circle. The kelpie's sting.

Dean's Adam's apple bobbed in his throat. "That thing—"

"His name is Ferry."

"I noticed a scar on its shoulder. It had me hypnotized, so Ava..."

"I already know everything," she said.

Dean explained anyway. "My father ordered us to follow the Crane River to your apartment and kill any monsters we saw on the way. He told us—or he told me, at least—he wanted us to clear the river of dangerous wildlife so we could safely bathe in it."

Cher told him the truth: his father suspected one of the kelpies in Salem was her familiar, and so he wanted them all dead.

"If I'd have known he was your friend, I never would have attacked," he said. "We shouldn't have anyway. They weren't hurting anyone." He looked up from his lap, where their hands were still intertwined. "I understand if you want to, um, to go our separate ways. I wouldn't blame Ferry if he doesn't want me around, and I wouldn't ask you to pick me over him."

Cher squeezed his shoulder. "Don't be silly," she said. "He won't hurt you."

"Are you sure?"

She hesitated, then nodded. "He'd have to kill me first, and he would never."

Not until your mother and father are dead and the ghosts of Salem are put to rest again. The words stuck in her throat. *Once they're gone, he's going to eat me. Then you should run far, far away.*

Instead she inched closer to Dean, leaned over, and did something she'd wanted to do to him for a long time. Something that wouldn't fix everything—or anything really—but at least it warmed her cold, cold bones.

She kissed him.

Chapter Twenty

Charity barely slept for twenty minutes. She jerked awake so violently she woke up Dean, who held her in his arms.

When she realized they were still lying on the bank of the Crane River, she relaxed.

Ferry was nowhere in sight. Still. How typical. She loved him to death, but he was such a flaky bastard. It would be a miracle if he ever actually arrived when he claimed he would.

Dean sat up beside her. "Are you alright? You should be sleeping." He reached out to touch her shoulder, a comforting gesture, but she ducked away from him.

"Yeah, y'know, that's a little easier said than done," she said. Then, softer, "I keep having nightmares."

Because of what Dean's father had put her through.

She didn't say it, but he read between the lines. He said nothing in response to her, and that was fine. He couldn't exactly apologize on behalf of his father when they both knew Bernard wasn't the least bit sorry for torturing her.

The sun began its slow ascent, turning the sky indigo. It would have been peaceful if only Cher could shake the Devourer's visions from her brain.

She's following you.

Cher turned to Dean. "Did you say something?"

"What? No." Again he asked, "Are you sure you're alright?"

"Not at all," she admitted.

She had heard a voice right in her ear. It was too soft to tell whether it was a man's or a woman's, to tell if it was someone's voice she knew.

She whipped around and saw the faintest cloud of mist hovering in the air behind her, so faint it was almost invisible under the sunlight.

A ghost. Not deathly gray and sinister like the spirits of the old trials, but one that glowed bright white. Fresh.

The Devourer's coming, Charity, the ghost whispered. *Think fast.*

And then the form vanished entirely.

The last time she'd seen the Devourer, it had crammed a vision into her mind—a body hanging from a tree, a wagon, an arm encircling her shoulders.

"Your mommy was a bad, bad person..."

"Oh, my God. Give me the grimoire." She held out a hand. Dean had taken the book back after they escaped, tucking it into his vest for safekeeping.

The vest was now in the grass, the book on top of it. He handed it to her, then put the vest back on—something he probably should have done before dozing off, no matter how uncomfortable it was to sleep in, just in case they had to run. They'd both let their guards down for that half hour, tangled up in each other.

Cher flipped to the summoning circles.

"This could go horribly, horribly wrong," she said to Dean. "I tried this once already and—well, it's how your father and those ghosts found me. But I won't mess up this time."

She quickly gathered stones from the riverbank and set them up in one circle, then another. Stepping into the first, she waved at Dean to join her.

"What are you doing?" he asked. "If this is dangerous, maybe we shouldn't—"

"We have to. Ferry protected us from the living, but he can't protect me from the dead. They're still hunting for us."

"Okay," said Dean, with the patience of a saint.

"Instead of waiting for them to sneak up on me, I'm going to set a trap. I know who the Devourer is."

"Right. I...don't. I don't even know what you're talking about."

"It's one of the spirits Bernard has working for him." Cher didn't deign to call him 'your father.' He didn't deserve that anymore. "Sorry, not 'it'—*she*. Except I don't think she's working for him willingly. I think he called her out of her peaceful rest and trapped her with some corrupt spell, some kind of curse. At least, that's how it sounded when Evelyn tried to explain the Devourer's nature to me."

Her mind worked overtime, but she knew every word she spoke was right. Those weren't just random snippets of the Trials hodge-podged together the Devourer had forced her to relive; they told a story.

One person's story.

"She was only a little girl," Cher said. "Practically a toddler. They searched her for strange bite marks and forced her to testify against her mother, to watch her mother hang." She pinched between her eyebrows, remembering something more. "Evelyn thought only the accusers had been reawakened, but she was wrong. There is one victim."

She grabbed Dean's arm, her eyes wide and bright.

"Those visions were never meant to be a threat," she said. "They were a cry for help!"

She turned to face the circle of stones opposite their own.

"Dorothy Good," she said, lifting her chin to greet the sunrise, "I break your chains and call upon thee! Meet me in these circles so I may set you free!"

Little Dorothy Good was only four years old when she was dragged into the dungeons and tortured until she testified against her own mother. She survived the Trials herself and grew up, a shadow of her former self, in quiet obscurity under the tender care of her father.

But when Bernard Winston called her spirit back from the Otherworld and bound her to his evil cause, it wasn't Dorothy's full-grown soul he had wanted; instead, he had forced her back into the tiny body of that terrified, helpless child teetering on the brink of madness.

Her tunic was plain, and stained with soot; her skin pale, with streaks of dirt. Shadows swirled around her with every move she made. Her eyes were a supernatural shade of icy blue, but from such a short distance Cher could see something else in them besides all the Devourer's hunger and frenzy—pain.

Only a couple of yards separated the two circles. Cher

crouched so she was on the same level as Dorothy and offered a friendly smile.

Of course, it wouldn't be that easy.

The humanity in Dorothy's eyes warped and vanished behind the Devourer's curse. Suddenly the child snarled and lunged at her circle's edge. A force-field sent her bouncing back to the circle's center, but that didn't stop her trying again and again like some caged, rabid monster.

"Not a monster," Cher said under her breath. "Not a monster. Just a little girl."

She stood again and took a step forward, over the stones of her own circle.

Dean reached for her wrist. "Cher?"

"Stay in the circle," she told him, tugging her wrist free of his grip.

"What's in the other circle?" he asked. Apparently he didn't take after his father. The dead were invisible to Dean.

"Just a little girl," she assured him. "Relax. I know what I'm doing."

"Do you?"

Nope. But it was a risk she needed to take.

Ferry would have his revenge; Cher would banish the other Salem ghosts when she was ready to face them. But this one deserved to be put back to rest gently, tucked in with a kiss on the forehead and a fairy tale.

The second she crossed into the Devourer's circle, Dorothy seized her hands in a vise-like grip and refused to let go, no matter how hard Cher pulled.

Together they fell through the shadows.

Up became down, down became up. Then Dorothy's memories came in rapid-fire succession: jangling shackles;

the prying hands, looking for those mysterious bite marks—she'd made them herself, it was a nervous habit. She chewed on her arms when she was scared. But they wouldn't listen, they wouldn't listen—they wanted her to say it was a witch's pet snake that did it; the cracking of whips; a hall packed full of people standing in silent judgment, staring with accusing glares; the death of the baby, Dorothy's little sister Mercy, so soon after she was born in that cursed jail cell; Dorothy's throat raw with screaming as she was ripped from Mommy's arms; sobs in the dark as Dorothy woke from another nightmare reliving the day Mommy was hanged.

The memories stalled and Cher returned to her own mind, her own body. She slumped to her knees.

Behind her she heard Dean call to her, sensed him taking a step towards her.

"Stay," she growled. "It isn't safe to step out of the circle."

"That's exactly why I'm worried about you," he said.

"I'm fine."

Then, turning back to Dorothy, she asked, "How long has it been since anyone has called you anything but 'Devourer'?"

The shadows around Dorothy, black and vicious, stilled. Cher brushed a loose strand of the little girl's hair from her blue, blue eyes.

"What a horrible name to give to such a sweet kid," she said. "That isn't you."

Something flashed in Dorothy's eyes, a wisdom beyond her years. Not the peaceful kind of wisdom, but the cynical kind. Her lip curled in a sneer.

Bernard's curse did not let go so easily.

"Give up," the girl said. "Evil will win anyway. It always does. Just stop. Stop trying to give me any hope, you fool. It's no use. You should know that better than anyone."

The shadows reared back and seized hold of Cher.

Another psychic onslaught came, this time not Dorothy's memories, but Cher's own. The children watching her trials with glee; the flames licking at her bare foot; the bullet piercing Sunny's chest; and Evelyn. Evelyn pacing and screaming and finally snapping, throwing her life away because she couldn't take it anymore.

Stones. Stones in Cher's pockets, sometimes smooth, sometimes jagged against her fingertips.

"Give up," the Devourer repeated.

When the shadows faded again, Cher found herself swaying on her feet. Her toe kicked a stone in the circle loose.

"Shit," she said.

"Charity?" Dean's voice called her back from the fog in her mind. "Talk to me, Cher."

The Devourer leapt for the hole in the circle, spotting her chance to escape.

But Cher was too quick. She grabbed Dorothy by the back of her collar, then took her hand. The child flailed and screamed an inhuman scream, not unlike the shriek Ferry made when he was angry or afraid.

"You're wrong," Cher said, holding Dorothy tight against her chest. "The world is always changing. Always getting better."

Dorothy tried and failed to elbow her in the gut. "Is it, though?" she said. "Is it really any different than it was a few months ago? Or three hundred years ago? Evil will win," she repeated. "It always comes back."

"So does love."

"No, it doesn't," Dorothy growled.

She assaulted Cher with more miserable memories—memories of the night Bates won the election, while the world looked on in shock and horror; the night eight years later when he announced he would be overstaying his term limits and continue ruling over America for the foreseeable future; all the fights with Maya when she begged Cher to go to protests with her and Cher begged her not to go lest she never come home; losing her dream job just months after getting it, and days later watching the zoo close its gates for good; the death of her mother; the news Bates was restricting travel and the realization she would probably never get to see her father again before he passed too; the morning she saw Dean's picture alongside state-sanctioned propaganda—the moment he chose his parents over her.

The constant threat of nuclear war.

The rise in hate crimes.

The shrugging of suit-clad shoulders at poverty, climate change, health crises.

The night the world ended, killing millions upon millions of people, and everything that had happened since.

So many times Cher's heart had been broken. So many times she had pieced it back together. So many times her love was tested.

But it hadn't failed her yet.

She smiled and shook her head, hugging Dorothy tighter.

Then Cher reached out with her mind and brushed the cobwebs away from the child's happier memories—the day the manacles were finally removed from her tiny, knobby wrists; hearing her father defend her to the monsters who locked her away in chains and hanged her poor mother unjustly and killed her baby sister with their negligence; the healing cups of tea her father made for her with love every day; mornings spent in companionable silence at the kitchen table, watching the sun rise through the window.

"I'm sorry," Cher whispered. "I am so sorry Bernard took your light from you. But he will not steal mine away too.

"Instead, I give you my love. And I give you my word I will go on fighting so no one ever suffers a fate like yours ever again. There's still hope for this world. I promise."

Dorothy stopped struggling. She was still for a moment before her tiny body shook with sobs. She twisted around and clung back at Cher, arms tight around her neck.

"Go, sweetheart," Cher said.

The shadows stopped swirling around Dorothy's feet. Her eyes faded to their original color, a rich, doleful brown, wide and maybe a little frightened.

But there was gratitude there too. Relief.

"I'm so sorry, Cher," she said, fading away. "I didn't mean to. It was the curse."

"I know. Get your rest."

"No, I'm not apologizing for all that." Dorothy pulled free of the hug. She was beginning to fade. "They heard me —the Devourer—they heard the Devourer scream after the circle broke. They're on their way. I'm sorry."

"What?"

Dorothy vanished.

Invading the space she'd occupied, hovering in her place, was the ghost of Samuel Parris.

He seized Cher by the throat.

* * *

Ferry heard the gunfire first, a hailstorm of bullets that startled the birds from the trees along the bank and sent rodents scurrying for the undergrowth.

Then he smelled the blood. Not faint, like the invisible thread emitted by the kelpie's mark on Dean's palm, but thick and oppressive. And it was in the water.

A head, a familiar *human* head without its body attached, bobbed past him, carried by the churning current.

Pulse roaring in his skull, he fought his way upriver.

The witch hunters couldn't possibly have found them. He'd been sure to cover all their tracks—

The ghosts drifted like vultures above the spot where he had left Cher. Below them, two figures were locked in battle on the shore, grappling over a weapon.

No. No!

* * *

Cher opened her eyes.

Beside her, a body, head-first in the river.

No—neck-first. There was no head left. The corpse wore a useless bulletproof vest.

From behind her came horrible, grinding, crunching sounds. A gurgling groan. Someone's dying breaths.

Nothing felt real. She could not look away from Dean's body. The mangled stump of his neck. His fingers reaching towards hers. The blood on her hands, all over her hands.

Her voice was a croak. "Did...I...?"

She pushed herself up just in time to vomit all over the riverbank.

The ghosts were gone. No Samuel Parris with his little daughter Betty, no Abigail Williams or Judge Cotton Mather.

Just Cher and this corpse and the nightmare noises behind her.

She turned slowly, slowly, somehow knowing deep in her heart exactly what she would see when she finally looked up.

Ferry stood over Bernard Winston, teeth digging at the man's throat.

"When...?" she said, barely a whisper. But the words wouldn't come. *When did he get here? What happened?*

There was an assault rifle strapped around Bernard's shoulders, bent at an odd angle just like the arms that held it. He was a mangled mess, just like his son.

But he was still alive. His eyes blinked, following Ferry's glowing esca bobbing overhead as the kelpie feasted.

"F-Ferry," Cher gasped. "*Ferry!*"

The kelpie froze. His snout was covered in blood, and bits of sinew and bone were stuck in his teeth.

"What happened?" she asked. "Dean's d-dead. I don't—know—how. I don't remember."

A bubble of blood popped in Bernard's throat. He lifted a weak, shaking finger and pointed it accusingly at Cher, then over to Dean's corpse. He tried to say something, but his voice box had been utterly destroyed long ago. His scarlet-stained lips shaped around a word.

You.

He smiled, showing a row of bloodstained teeth. Then a rattling breath shook his body. His hand dropped back to his side and his fingers curled into fists as a spasm racked him head to toe. His eyes widened.

They didn't close even after his life finally left him.

Cher took a staggering step backwards. *You.* There was only one way to interpret that.

Hands. All she could see in her mind's eye were hands. Parris's, lunging for her. Dean's, stretched out to her. Bernard's, accusing her. Her own hands, red, red, red with Dean's blood.

What had she done while she was under Parris's control?

Cher shook her head. Her knees trembled and almost gave out, but Ferry was there for her to lean on. Ferry, covered in bits and pieces of Bernard. She gripped his mane so tight she could have pulled a clump of it out.

"Was he telling the truth?" she said. "Did you see what happened? Did I—did I kill him?"

Ferry tried to reach out to her with magic, to ease her mind with an illusion. He hadn't seen, no. And she couldn't remember. But if he planted a false memory for her, maybe it would bring her peace. Maybe—

He hissed and sidestepped away from Cher, but she held fast to his mane.

"W-what's wrong?" she said.

"Nothing," Ferry lied. "Just a stomachache is all. Must have eaten too fast."

He couldn't break through to her mind.

Whatever had happened to her here, the trauma had driven her over the brink. Her thoughts were a jagged, scrambled mess. It felt like reaching into a fire, trying to calm her.

He thought of Sunny and Evelyn. Was this what the last few weeks had been like for the phoenix? Watching helplessly as his witch wandered somewhere far, far out of his reach?

Suddenly Cher's hand on his neck pushed him away and she leapt back. He turned to face her.

"Cher?" he said.

"It was you," she said. "It was you!" She lurched forward again and beat her small fists against his side. "You killed him! You killed Dean!"

"What?"

"Are you happy?" she sneered. "You got your revenge." Her lank hair fell across her face. She clawed it away, leaving a welt across the bridge of her own nose. "But I'm not falling for it. You thought you could trick me into thinking it was someone else's fault. Bernard's, or the ghosts'—or mine! What did you do to me? *What did you* do *to me?*"

She got right up in his face. He backed up a few steps.

"Charity," he said, trying to stay calm and reasonable, "that isn't what happened."

"Then what *did?*"

"I don't know. I wasn't here. I came back upriver to find you and Bernard fighting. You were...not yourself. I tried reaching out to you, but your mind was blank." He nodded to the stones in the dirt, half-circles now, kicked apart in all the commotion. "What happened here, Cher? Before Bernard arrived? Maybe we can piece everything together."

"I-I wanted to set Dorothy free." Her voice was thick with tears.

"Dorothy?"

"The Devourer." A smile stretched her lips. "It worked. She can rest again." Then just as quickly the smile vanished. "But the circle b-broke..."

Ferry could have kicked himself. She had warned him. *Things never go well when we separate...*

He should have listened. Dammit, she was like a toddler he couldn't leave alone for more than two seconds, and—

He stamped down his anger and fear, focusing instead on the matter at hand.

After Cher took care of the Devourer, the other Salem ghosts had arrived, attracted by all the psychic energy. And they had brought Bernard with them.

"Why didn't you wait for me to come back?" he said, not unkindly. "Maybe I could have protected you."

"I was so careful this time. And Dean was with me. Dean..."

Just saying his name sent the world spinning around her again. Without meaning to, she glanced in his direction. The head, the head. It was just...gone. She couldn't have done that. Could she? Not with her bare hands...

She had attacked Ava with super-human strength...

No. It could have been an assault rifle, bullet after bullet after bullet after bullet ripping holes in the throat until the head rolled right off the body.

Or it could have been a monster's teeth, pulling the head clean off the neck...

She swayed on her feet. Ferry inched closer, hoping to

stop her from falling. But she recoiled, preferring to stagger a few more times rather than touch him.

He stared at her. Whatever bond they had had was quickly turning to dust and blowing away in the wind. He had to stop it.

"I didn't do it, Cher," he said. "Please believe me."

Silence. She stared at the ground, fists balled up in the skirt of her blood-stained shift. A tear dripped off the tip of her nose.

Look at me, he wanted to beg her. *Please look at me.*

"I need you to leave me alone," she said.

A whimper sounded in the kelpie's throat, soft and pathetic.

"I don't think that's a good idea. You're not—"

She cut him off, squeezing her eyes shut as she spoke. "Please just leave me alone."

"D-do you want me to find you later on, or—"

"*Leave!*" she roared, finally looking at him, and now all he wanted was for her to look away. It broke his heart to be on the receiving end of that dagger-glare.

"As you wish," he said, ducking his head as he approached the Crane River. "Cher, I-I will be right here if —when—you need me again."

Please come back.

She did not answer, only turned and dashed into the trees.

Chapter Twenty-One

For the third night in a row, Maya Ambrose dreamed of a fairy godmother. Not the quaint, plump kind from Cinderella, but a sneaky one.

This fairy godmother took the form of the creepy witch in the mural painted on the attic wall in the Olmsteads' old house. She knew it was meant to be a touching gift for Charity on the day she outgrew her toddler's bed, but there was something too uncanny valley in the way Teddy and Ros painted that lady's face.

After hours and hours of staring at it, Maya realized what it was—the eyes. The shading around the chin and the cheeks and the nose was amazing, even perfect, but the eyes looked fake. Unfinished. Dead.

She wished she had some paint to cover it up.

In the dreams, the fairy godmother knocked on the screen door and waited for Maya to answer. When she did, the godmother blew fairy dust in her face, blinked those creepy, painted eyes at her, pointed northwest, and disappeared with a meow.

Yes, a meow. Alistair always sensed when her dreams were in borderline nightmare territory, so he'd yowl at her and poke his mushy little paw at her face until she woke up.

Except this night, the dream ended with a hiss and a bang.

Maya started awake.

She'd been asleep on the living room floor. The rest of the coven—Anton, Sara, and Nat—were crashing at the house. She'd sent Alistair off to summon them to discuss the news Cher brought of the witch hunters in Danvers, so she and Juliet had offered them all beds.

Juliet was on the couch, her eyes open too. She pressed a finger to her lips.

Tense, she reached underneath her pillow for the kitchen knife she kept there, sprang up, and pointed her weapon at the door.

A woman dressed in a bloody linen shift stood there.

"I'm home," the intruder said, smiling the kind of smile a psychopath would give before swinging at their victim with an axe.

But the glint of an axe blade never came. The woman leaned back against the door—it was the door slamming shut that must have woken Maya, she knew they should have locked it—and peered right through Juliet like she wasn't even there.

"Mom?" the intruder called. "Dad?"

No answer. Her face crumpled.

"Mom? Dad?" she said again, louder this time.

"Maya?" Juliet didn't take her eyes off the intruder as she asked over her shoulder, "Is that *Cher?*"

It was hard to tell through the blood smeared all over

the woman's face, but Juliet was right. This stranger wasn't a stranger at all.

"Charity?" Maya took a step around the couch; slowly, as if she were approaching a rabid dog.

The woman's eyes snapped into focus, locking on her.

"I don't like this," Juliet said. Alistair, who stood with his back arched on the arm of the sofa, growled in agreement.

Maya shushed them both.

Footsteps thundered down the attic staircase and through the bedroom hallway. Nat, Sara, and Anton appeared, Sara holding a pistol at the ready.

Cher saw the gun and yelped, throwing a protective arm up over her face.

"Charity," Maya said again, sharper this time, to keep the woman's attention on her, "it's me." She spread her arms, a gesture of welcome, and positioned herself so she blocked the gun from Cher's view.

Cher lowered her arm just enough to peek at Maya. Then a little more, and a little more, until she relaxed completely.

Maya closed the space between them, touched a gentle hand to Charity's shoulder, then pulled her into a hug.

Charity glimpsed something behind Maya and suddenly ducked past her.

Alistair. She was headed straight for the damned cat.

He growled, but Charity paid no mind. Maya shot the cat a mom look, eyebrows raised, finger pointing in a warning. *Be nice.*

She's covered in blood! the cat protested.

Be. Nice.

His fur flattened. Disgusted at the dried blood under

Charity's nails, he curled a lip. After this he'd have to bathe himself all day to feel clean again.

"Charity." Maya approached carefully, sidling around so she was in Charity's peripheral vision and not sneaking up behind her. "Cher, tell me what happened." She placed both hands on Cher's shoulders and helped her stand up straight.

From the hallway, Nat whispered to the others, "Hold up—did she say 'Charity'?"

A flashlight clicked on and the rest of the Coven Kids stepped fully into the living room.

Charity smiled and shielded her eyes from the flashlight's glare. "Oh! Hey, everyone. Wow. Look at you all. It's been so long!"

"Y-yeah," said Anton, forcing a friendly tone, "we, uh...we sailed up here in my boat because Maya said you'd stopped by. We're, um...happy to see you."

The others gave overenthusiastic nods and muttered in agreement.

"Cher," said Maya, "Jules and I were worried sick about you. You just disappeared the other morning without saying goodbye. Alistair woke us up and told us you wandered off? With a ghost?"

Charity's expression remained blank.

"He said he met your familiar. A kelpie?"

A frown flitted across Cher's face at the mention of the creature.

"The kelpie mentioned Danvers. We suspected the worst. So, when the others got here, we started brainstorming a plan..."

Her voice trailed off.

Tears pooled in Charity's eyes. "You're all so kind. I'm sorry. I'm sorry I wasn't a better friend to you all."

"Cher, sweetie, that's behind us now. What—what happened to you? What's going on? Please."

"What do you mean?" The smile remained plastered to Charity's face even as the first tears fell.

Maya took Cher's hands in her own, turning them over. The blood was long dried, flaking off.

"What is all this? Are you hurt?"

"No, silly." Charity yanked her hands free with a little too much force. "I'm fine." She reached again for Alistair, almost obsessively running her fingers through his fur. Her broken nails nicked his skin and he snapped a warning at her; she didn't flinch, only muttered an apology and buried her nose in his fur.

Juliet came up beside Maya. "She needs help," she whispered into her ear. "Looks like she's in shock. We're not gonna get any information out of her like this."

Their visitor abruptly turned to the fireplace and crouched in front of it. "It's chilly in here," she said, and light flared to life in her hands.

A fireball. She had a fucking fireball.

"Okay!" said Maya, clapping her hands together. "Cher, how about we get you to bed? You look like you could use some rest."

"That sounds nice."

The fireball vanished and she headed for the attic stairs; Anton stepped aside to let her through, glancing warily at Maya.

Of course, Charity wanted her old bedroom. Anton would just have to find somewhere else to sleep.

Fine, this is fine, Maya thought, following her up to the attic.

She climbed right into the twin-size bed.

Fully aware of everyone else hovering in the doorway at her back, Maya crossed the room and wrestled the blankets out from underneath Charity, tucking her in like a child.

"I have to tell you something," Cher whispered. Her smile had vanished.

"Sure. What is it?"

Her forehead wrinkled, like she couldn't remember what she'd meant to say.

Then, "I saw Danvers," she said. "You need to hide."

Danvers. Northwest. Maya felt the painted eyes of the witch in the mural staring down at them.

"Did you get my note?"

"Your—? You mean this?"

Maya fumbled in the pocket of her blouse and pulled out the wrinkled page she assumed Cher had torn from Evelyn's grimoire, with the illusion spell scribbled on it.

The sight of the handwriting put Charity at ease. She inhaled for what seemed like the first time since she'd arrived at the house, exhaled slow, and reached to press Maya's fist closed around the illusion spell.

"Do that now. You should have done it ages ago." She stifled a yawn. "Quickly. Before the hunters find you."

"But we can't," Maya protested.

"Don't worry about where it came from. Evelyn's spellbook was never cursed. I tried a summoning spell, and I'm fine! See? Not dead. It's safe. I promise."

A summoning spell? So that must be where that ghost came from, the one Charity vanished with.

"We—" Maya began, but Charity wasn't listening. Her eyes had already drifted closed, and her breathing turned slow and even.

A shiver crept down Maya's spine. She was careful not to look up again at the mural as she stood and exited the room, but even so, she felt the painted eyes burning holes in her back.

* * *

Cher never really fell asleep.

In a moment of clarity, she realized Maya and the others would never cast the illusion spell, leaving them all in danger.

She would have to come up with a solution herself. Perhaps she could find a way to cast the spell on her own.

But she couldn't think straight, as long as Maya bombarded her with questions. So she'd faked sleep until she heard the attic door creak shut, and then listened for everyone's footsteps down the stairs.

Those footsteps never came. Instead, Cher heard hushed whispers on the staircase. She sat up in bed, tip-toed across the room, and crouched in front of the door.

The flashlight shone under the crack between the door and the hardwood floor. She imagined them all sitting out there, keeping watch over her.

No, no, no. They weren't supposed to be worrying about *her*. She was fine. They had to make the house invisible *now*. Nora was still alive. Nora and Ava. And they would want revenge when they discovered Bernard was dead. That Dean...that Dean was...

Cher stuffed a fist into her mouth to stop herself sobbing.

"...think she's going to be okay?" It was Juliet's voice just outside the door.

"I have no idea," Maya replied. "Anton? You're the one who went to medical school. You got any input?"

An exasperated sigh, a little further down the stairs. "Mental health wasn't my specialty," he said. "Sorry. But I think Juliet's right. She's in shock. Something must have traumatized her."

"What do you think happened?" Sara asked.

"I can't even begin to imagine," Maya said. "All that blood... Maybe we should've offered her a swim in the ocean before we put her to bed? To clean herself off?"

"Not at this time of night," said Nat. "First thing in the morning."

"I feel so bad for her," said Juliet.

Cher felt a flare of annoyance. She didn't need their pity. She needed them to listen to her. She reached for the doorknob—

"She left us this," Maya said, and Cher heard the wrinkled page from Evelyn's grimoire unfolding. "She just told me the hunters are coming, and we need to hide."

"Wish she'd given us an easier spell," said Juliet. "Think we should try it again? Third time's the charm?"

What? Cher leaned closer against the door. They *had* tried the illusion spell?

"No way," said Anton. "Last thing I need is you two passing out again. That was a nightmare."

Yes, yes way, Cher thought, grinding her teeth.

"You have to do it!" she yelled at the door.

A pause. No doubt they were all exchanging glances

with one another, judging her, shaking their heads because she was just too much, too crazy. Why wouldn't they listen to her?

The door swung open. There stood the Coven Kids, all staring at her.

It was Anton who stepped forward first.

"Cher," he said, "the spell is too powerful, even for all of us working together. Hiding a trinket is one thing, but a whole house? Come on. We're strong, but we're not *that* strong."

He gave a nervous laugh. No one laughed with him.

"Please, rest," he said. "You need to give yourself a break."

Cher backed away from him, stumbling over her own feet. "No," she said. "Let me help you! I can help you cast the spell."

"One more witch won't make a difference," Sara said. "A house this size, I think we'd need a whole other coven. Maybe two."

"Then, Anton—Maya said you were staying in a trailer. What if you hid that?"

He glanced at the others. "I mean...we could try..." he said.

"I think the spell is just beyond our skill level," Sara said in an apologetic tone.

"Please." The backs of Cher's knees hit the twin bed. She fell back onto it, catching the edge of the mattress to keep herself upright. "Please. You don't understand. There are hunters, *witch* hunters, up in Danvers. They're on their way. They'll kill—they'll kill—!"

They'll kill you all too.

Cher did not see Juliet and Maya nod to each other.

She did not notice Juliet slip a vial from her pajama pocket, did not see her drip a little of the vial's contents onto her thumb.

Cher did not dodge quickly enough when Juliet swooped down and took the back of her head in one hand, tipped it back, and brushed the thumb against her lips.

The potion tasted warm and sweet, like a mug of chamomile tea with a drop of honey. No—like cinnamon sugar. No...like cotton candy...

And then Cher slept.

The others arranged her more comfortably in bed. Pity and shame silenced them as they worked to fluff the pillow, lay her down, and pull the covers back up to her chin.

Maya brushed Cher's hair out of her eyes.

"Anton, prepare the boat," she said over her shoulder.

She'd been afraid of this moment. They had all been afraid of it. But none of them were surprised. This—what they'd built here—it was too good to last.

An after-world this full of magic, someone was bound to blame it on witches like them.

Juliet's voice was small. "But Salem's our home."

"Yeah." Maya's jaw tightened. "We can't take it back from them if we're dead, though. We leave for the island at dawn."

* * *

It was still dark when Cher awoke. She feared for a second she was back in the cell, shackles around her wrists and ankles. But she could move. Thank God, she could move.

She threw off the covers and slipped out of bed.

Maya and Juliet were on the floor at the foot of the bed,

snoring soundly. Light as the shadows, Cher leaned over Maya and reached into her blouse pocket, plucking out the illusion spell's instructions.

She glanced at the attic window and saw on the glass a rune traced in dark, dried blood she hadn't noticed before.

So the coven really had tried the spell. Why hadn't it worked?

No worries. Cher had really powerful blood in her own veins. Evelyn and Bernard had both said so. The blood of not one, but two powerful psychics. If Maya and the others weren't strong enough, Cher could just mingle her blood with theirs and finish up the spell herself. Right?

With her sharp canine teeth, she bit into her fingertip hard enough to draw blood. Her eyes watered with pain as she ripped a chunk of skin loose.

First, the attic window and door. Stepping carefully over the creaky spots on the floor, she climbed onto her bed and smeared her blood on the window's glass, tracing right over the rune from the Coven Kids' attempt.

When she reached the door, she hesitated. It always stuck. She'd have to pull hard to get it open, and no doubt it would creak on its hinges. When she'd lived here with her parents and they slept in the master bedroom on the opposite side of the house, the noise wasn't a problem. But with two of Cher's unwelcome guardians up here in the attic with her, she didn't know how she could escape without alerting them.

The magic in her chest, activated by the first step of the illusion spell, pulsed as if to remind her of its use.

Right. First things first. She traced over the bloody rune the Coven Kids had left—a mark underneath the keyhole.

Then she took the doorknob in her hand and thought, *Shh. Shhh.*

As was her will, the door opened smooth as butter, without a sound.

She drifted down the stairs like a silent ghost and turned right. One rune on the bathroom door and the small window inside. Another on the kitchen's swinging door, the door leading out onto the back porch, and the big bay window that overlooked the Atlantic Ocean.

She stopped for half a second to admire the beautiful view, then turned back down the hallway.

As she passed the master bedroom, where Nat and Sara slept, she repeated the hushing spell and sneaked inside. They tossed and turned in their sleep. It was like playing Red Light, Green Light, the way Cher froze each time they shifted.

Eventually she made it to the window and left another streak of her blood, doing the same to the door on her way out of the room.

Finally, the living room.

Anton was asleep on the couch, Alistair curled in front of the embers dying in the fireplace.

Stay asleep, Cher silently pleaded with the cat. She couldn't have the little tattletale running upstairs to wake Maya and letting her know what she was doing. She could just imagine the lecture she would get. *Are you insane? You can't do it alone. You'll wear yourself out!*

But Maya would see. They'd all see.

Alistair's paws twitched. He was out of it, deep in kitten dreams.

A floorboard creaked under her foot. She froze as Anton sat up.

"Who'zair?" he grumbled into the dark.

Cher pressed herself to the wall, willing the shadows to embrace her.

It worked. He didn't see her.

"Stupid old house," he muttered, flopping back and throwing a pillow over his head. She didn't have to wait long until he started snoring again.

Two windows, one on either side of the front door. Then the front door itself, which she opened so she could complete the finishing touch outside, well out of Anton's earshot.

She drew the final rune and unfolded the instructions again. The last step said to recite a few words in Latin. Cher didn't understand them, but that was fine. Even as her lips formed the unfamiliar syllables, she knew she was pronouncing them correctly. The magic in her chest burned hotter.

She shut her eyes, lifted her chin, and whispered the last two words with confidence.

When she opened her eyes, nothing happened.

The fire in her chest went out, like someone had thrown a bucket of water over it, and there was no cue, no hazy force-field, no spark from her fingertips, no glow around the runes, to indicate whether the spell had worked.

"Dammit."

Wasn't her blood enough?

She smacked herself on the forehead. *Of course not.*

She was missing a crucial element. A witch a nothing without her familiar by her side, boosting her powers.

And Cher's familiar just so happened to specialize in illusion magic, like the kind this spell required.

"Blood," she said under her breath. "Blood. Right. I just need a little bit of blood. It's the least he can do, after—well. Just a little blood."

She fled down the front porch steps, her shift giving off a ghostly glow in the moonlight.

* * *

Maya woke before the sun did. Stretching off her sleepiness, she twisted around and looked at the twin bed in the corner.

It was empty.

She jerked up. "Jules," she said, shaking her wife's shoulder. "Juliet, wake up."

Bless her, Juliet's eyes opened without complaint. Always so instinctively protective, even in her sleep.

"What is it?" she asked, sitting up too.

"Charity's gone."

They both jumped up and headed for the door.

When they saw the bloody streak on the doorknob, and fresh blood traced over their own rune, they both froze in their tracks.

Maya reached into her blouse pocket and found nothing. The slip of paper with the invisibility spell on it was gone.

"Oh, no."

They hurried downstairs and found more wet blood on the other doors, all the windows.

How had none of them heard her? Not even Alistair.

Maya woke the rest of the coven and together they

checked the back lawn, the front lawn, hoping to find foot-prints in the mud or even drops of blood, any hint to tell them which way Charity had gone.

But they found no signs of her anywhere.

Maya bit back tears. That damn spell had drained her and Juliet of nearly all their magical energy. They were lucky they hadn't ended up in comas. And that was *with* everyone else's help.

"The good news is, we haven't found a body," said Anton, as they climbed to the front porch. "So we can all relax a little."

With perfect timing, a gun fired somewhere in the distance, startling them all. A flock of magpies scattered.

Next to Maya, Juliet counted the birds carefully. "Thir-teen," she said.

"For the devil himself." Sara held a hand up over her eyes, warding off evil. "Maya...I hate to say it, but I think we need to go. That could be—"

A bullet struck the first step of the porch. Far up the road, the light of the rising sun glinted off the weapons of at least a dozen armed men and women—guns and knives and crossbows. They strolled at a leisurely pace, like killers in a horror film toying with their victims.

"Shit!" Maya shouted as she swung the door open and shepherded everyone inside. "*Fuck!*"

"We have to leave," said Sara. She waved Anton and Nat over to the couch, gesturing for them to help her use it to block the door.

"Without Charity?" said Nat.

Maya puffed up her cheeks and blew out a breath, still fending off tears. To herself, she mumbled, "Was she even really here?"

The last twelve hours seemed like some weird feverish nightmare, one in which their perfect little sanctuary crumbled to dust.

"What if Cher's out there?" she asked the others. "What if they find her?"

"Honey, we're sitting ducks here," Juliet said, rubbing her back.

"Cher's smart," said Sara. "And scared, after whatever happened to her. She's in flight mode. If she's out there, I'm sure she heard the gunshots. She'll hide until we can come back for her."

"Right," said Anton. "If we escape now, we can come back and rescue her once we've thrown the hunters off our trail. But if we stay, we're dead."

"It's like you said, honey," said Juliet. "We can't take Salem back if we're dead."

"They have assault rifles, Maya," said Nat. "They caught us off guard. We have to go."

She shook her head. They were right, but she was terrified and confused and leaving Cher behind just felt wrong. That woman needed their help.

"We could use the elemental spells," she said, "the ones I told you about—"

"None of us but you and Juliet know how to do them yet," said Sara. "We might burn the whole house down. We might hurt each other."

"But—"

"There's no time." Juliet gave her hand a reassuring squeeze. "Cher's one of us. We'll come back for her."

A bullet broke the window and embedded itself in the fireplace. Everyone threw themselves onto the floor.

"Fine," Maya said. "Okay. This isn't the end."

The coven would come back. And when they did, they'd find Cher again and welcome her back into their fold, and together they would remind those bastards out there Salem belonged to the witches.

"Let's go," Maya said to her coven. "Fast."

Thank goddess the weather was all right for sailing. They would have no problem escaping quickly to nearby Great Misery island, where Anton had been storing supplies for his fishing trips.

Together they worked, quiet and quick as lightning, to pack the boat with their spellbooks and some extra food they had grabbed in the rush out the back door.

Last of all, they placed Alistair inside. He curled up under one of the benches, ears flat against his head.

"Hey," said Juliet, rapping her knuckles against the side of the boat, "do any of y'all have it in you to try that spell one last time? I think we could pull it off with this little thing."

She was right. It was only a small fishing boat, almost too small for all five of them.

With one of her earrings, Maya pricked everyone's fingers. Then she hopped into the boat, and together they used their blood to trace a protective rune five times into the boat's front bench, then onto both oars.

They'd attempted Evelyn's illusion spell so many times they had the Latin memorized. Joining hands, they all recited it as quickly and clearly as possible, pouring all their hearts into the willpower they shared between them.

With the last syllable spoken, they opened their eyes and the magic splashed over them like a wave.

The world around the boat pulsed and then went still, and they knew the invisibility shield was in place.

"We did it!" Nat said, hugging Sara so hard he almost knocked her out of the boat.

"Holy shit," Anton breathed.

They rested a little easier now, knowing the hunters wouldn't see them.

Maya caught Juliet's wrist as she moved to shift the boat offshore with one of the oars.

"What if we waited?" she said. "Now that the hunters won't see us. I just—I feel like I'm failing her." She pressed her lips tightly together, trying to hold back the tears welling up in her eyes. "I have such a horrible feeling. She needs someone. She needs *us*—"

But Sara put a finger to her lips and pointed at the back of the house.

Half of the hunters swept the backyard, looking for any sign of escapees. A few of them were headed down to the shore.

"Does this thing still hide us if they accidentally bump into it?" Nat whispered, hardly moving his lips.

No one had the answer.

We have to go, Juliet mouthed, looking just as pained and sorry as Maya felt.

And so, they shoved off.

"I'm so sorry," Maya said under her breath, as if Cher might hear her. "But I promise we'll come back for you. Just wait. Please, please just wait."

They hadn't gotten far when Juliet said between oar-strokes, "Do you smell that?"

Her face was grim. Everyone sniffed.

Smoke.

The hunters had set the house on fire.

* * *

Please just wait, Cher silently prayed to the Coven Kids. *I'll be right back. You all just go on sleeping and let me do this for you. Everything will be fine. I promise.*

She followed the banks of the Crane River back to the spot where it all began, back to where she first met Ferry.

She wouldn't need to say sorry. Just like he always did, Ferry would know just by looking at her exactly what was on her mind. He'd sense her shame and accept it as an apology for the way she'd lashed out at him.

Of course, he hadn't killed Dean. How stupid she'd been to think so. It was Bernard. It had to be Bernard.

They would hug it out and then Ferry would pick up on Cher's panic and do whatever she needed. She only needed a little blood, just a tiny, tiny drop, and the spell would work.

Dean's body lay on the shore. She pretended it wasn't him—easy to do when he had no face—and removed the machete from his belt.

Just a *little* blood.

"Cher?"

Ferry stood a few feet up the shore. He'd been pushing a stone with his nose.

Only then did Cher notice the pile of rocks against Dean's left side. Ferry must have been building a cairn so he wouldn't have to stare at the body every day.

Or, more likely, out of respect for Cher. He could have just eaten Dean's corpse, but he hadn't.

She smiled. "Ferry," she said, walking towards him.

The kelpie was pleasantly surprised to see her, but she walked strangely, arms behind her back.

"Cher, I'm so glad you're here," he said. "I wanted to tell you before, but there wasn't time. I canceled our contract. You're free."

She didn't answer him, only kept approaching.

Ferry tossed his head nervously and took a step backwards, but she reached out and tangled her fingers in his mane.

"What are you doing, Cher?" he said, unable to hide the fear in his voice.

"I only need a little," she said insistently, raising the machete she'd hidden behind her back.

He tried to yank his head free, but she held fast.

"Ferry, stand *still!*" she said. "It won't hurt if you just—"

He did not want to hurt her. He did not mean to hurt her. But she wouldn't stop, she wouldn't *stop*—so he reared up and kicked, just as she swung the machete.

This was what he deserved, the bite of the blade in his throat. For hurting her like this.

Forgive me. He couldn't tell which of them thought those words. *Forgive me.*

The last thing he saw was his own blood showering Charity as she fell away from him, limp as a precious doll.

Chapter Twenty-Two

Charity's head didn't feel right—in more ways than one. She groaned and sat up, pressing a hand against her skull.

Her fingers came away slick with blood.

Not just her hand. Everything. Everything was covered in blood.

"P-plenty," she said. Her teeth chattered. "Th-this will do."

She stood and staggered back down the riverbank, stepping over Dean and Ferry where they lay on the shore, as if they were only logs in her way.

She did not look back.

The sun still hung in the sky, but she felt so cold. Her tongue tasted of metal and her shift stuck to her skin.

Not to worry, not to worry, for she had everything she needed to save her friends.

She whistled as she picked her way back through Salem, imagining the looks of awe the Coven Kids would wear once she finished the spell. They'd be so impressed, so proud. So safe. They could live happily ever after together in her favorite place in the world. It would be a tight fit with the six of them, sure, and Ferry wouldn't be able to fit inside at all, but that was a small price to pay for a fairy tale life.

Everything was falling into place. She had the power to protect her friends, Bernard Winston was gone, and Ferry had canceled the contract. The memory was vague and distant like a dream, but she did recall hearing him say that as she asked to borrow just a pinch of his blood. She remembered throwing her arms around him and thanking him, then teasing him about being such a big softy. She remembered the way he nudged his hideously adorable nose against her palm. She remembered thinking how perfect it all was.

He couldn't live in the house, no, but he could stay where the Crane River emptied into the sea, only a short walk away. He'd visit her every day. The others might be a little afraid of him at first, but she would show them how kind he was and eventually he would fit right in. He was sure to become great friends with Alistair. They were both little shits.

Oh, how cozy it would be!

When she arrived at the arcade, she noticed the thick, black cloud drifting across the sky.

Memories of the Devourer came rushing back to her and she flinched, but then she caught the scent of smoke and heard a thundering crash in the distance. She heard a wolfish howl, a burst of laughter carried on the wind.

And gunfire, *powpowpowpowpow.*

Please, no.

Her vision blurred with tears as she stumbled through the flooded neighborhood, the ocean water splashing all around her and rinsing her clean of all that precious blood. But she knew before she reached the house her worst fear had come true.

She was too late.

* * *

"You okay, Mrs. Winston?" one of the witch hunters asked.

Nora stood with her arms crossed at the base of the hill, watching the house collapse in on itself. It had been burning for a couple of hours. She thought she should have felt something—joy, perhaps—but instead she frowned.

"How many witches did you say you counted on that front porch, Ava?" she asked her niece, who had insisted on being put in charge of the search party Bernard had sent out after the trials.

"Five," Ava responded.

"Then why," Nora said, calm at first, then escalating, "don't I smell any *burning flesh?*"

To her credit, Ava didn't wince. "We searched the perimeter and found no survivors, no trails," she scowled. "All of them went inside and none of them came back out. I promise you those witches are dead. Maybe your sense of smell is wearing out in your old age, *auntie dearest.*"

In the same second Nora smacked Ava across the face, Ava's hair went up in flames.

She screamed a horrible, ear-shattering wail that filled the entire neighborhood, grabbing at the sides of her head as if to rip her hair out rather than feel the flames licking her skull.

Instead, her sleeves caught fire. She fell to her knees in agony.

Behind her stood a monster—a ghoulish being with a misshapen head, a bit of brain showing where hair and flesh had broken away. The thing was coated in blood and dirt, and there were symbols streaked through the mess all over its face and arms and legs. In either palm it wielded a ball of fire, and its eyes were pure white.

Ava crumpled into a burning ball at Nora's feet.

The sky turned rapidly black, too fast, as if it were on a time lapse. Lightning flashed, punctuating the screams of the rest of the search party. Each panicked bullet fired at the beast missed its mark.

Nora could have sworn one of the bullets changed its course mid-flight, inches away from the monster's face, as if it had glanced off a shield.

The air reeked of human flesh. They were all dead. Ava and her soldiers.

Yet Nora was sure she had only blinked a few times. How? How did it kill so fast? Surely this was a nightmare.

The monster came to a halt before her. Its eyes returned to their natural color, gray-blue. Human eyes.

Overhead, the storm calmed.

"How does it feel?" asked Charity Olmstead. "Knowing you failed?"

Nora knew the bitch had killed her family. A scout had brought word to her earlier that morning Bernard had never returned to Danvers, and they'd found his body with Dean's on the bank of the Crane River.

The fools. She'd tried to warn them Olmstead would be the death of them.

But now Cher's voice was weak and tired. Dying. Whatever hellish power had flooded her veins just moments ago was gone, spent. She was a dead battery.

Nora could kill her and get revenge, but that was no fun without the challenge. She was already dead.

"You tell me," she said instead, smiling and pointing up at the house. It was a ruin of ashes and embers now.

No, Olmstead's friends were *not* in the house. They couldn't have been. They would have screamed.

But let her believe they were. Let her bear all the agony.

Turning her back, Nora sank into the satisfaction of knowing she had won.

She was so relaxed and smug she didn't start when something pinched the back of her neck; didn't even realize at first a blade protruded from the front of her throat. Not until the ground rose up to meet her and the world slipped away, and it was too late to curse Charity Olmstead's name.

* * *

Cher held both her hands in front of her face.

Whose blood was this? How many lives had she taken?

Her breath hitched in her throat.

What have I done? All for nothing.

Evelyn and Ferry and Maya and her friends—they were all dead. Because of her.

She stood and ran, stumbling her way through the neighborhood, which was now calm and sunny as if a magical storm hadn't just passed through. The sunlight glared, too bright, too unforgiving.

She needed shadows. Shadows were safe for the likes of her. Where were all the shadows?

But there was nowhere to hide, nowhere to hide.

Chapter Twenty-Three

When the colt heard the footsteps shuffling in the underbrush behind him, he knew it would be her. His mate tensed beside him.

"Want me to take care of this?"

"No," said the colt. "Let me."

He had thought long and hard about what his sire would want in this moment, and though his own heart hungered for revenge, well...look where such a hunger had gotten them all.

With an affectionate nibble at his late sire's ear, the colt stood and turned to greet the witch who had done this.

Charity Olmstead lurched out of the bushes covered in blood, no doubt some of it his sire's. There was a deep and ugly wound on the side of her scalp and she walked like a filly, unsteady on her legs. Wincing in the glaring sun, she threw up an arm to shield her eyes and scanned the river.

"Ferry?" she said, looking right through the colt and his mate, right through his sire's corpse.

Ferry. The name stirred something in the colt's chest, but he did not know who Ferry was.

"What will you do?" his mate asked.

The colt shook his head just slightly, but it was enough the glint of his esca captured Charity Olmstead's attention. Her gaze locked onto it. She came to a standstill and her expression went blank.

He sifted through her memories, or tried to. Her mind was a jumbled mess of pain and terror.

But in the midst of it all, he managed to find the image of a cliff overlooking the Atlantic, a pod of whales surfacing in the distance.

And his sire's voice, gentle and concerned, *"Why are you crying?"*

"I wish M-Mom and Dad were here," the witch wept. *"I wish they could see this."*

A wish was all the colt needed. He pulled out of her mind and glanced back at his mate.

"Just so we're clear," he said, "I'm not doing this for her."

And yet, he remembered the force of his sire's love for this human, the little spark of it he'd felt himself the last time the two of them spoke. That same feeling tugged at him now. This was his sire's kindred spirit. How could he not love her? Or pity her, at the very least.

"Sure you're not," his mate taunted him. Then, more softly, "It's okay. I understand."

Of course he did. Their hearts were one.

Grant her mercy, Little One.

And so the colt offered her all her heart desired. Or at least an illusion of it.

She strode slowly, sleepily, towards him and climbed up into his saddle.

* * *

When Cher stepped out of the bushes, she found Ferry right where she left him, waiting in the river for her to return.

Impossible. She could have sworn...

Yet the blood was all gone and there he stood, ugly and lovely as ever.

"Ferry!" she cried, running to greet him. She placed both hands on either side of his face and planted a big kiss on his rotten nose. "Oh, Ferry, you're okay! I had the most horrible nightmare."

"It's okay now," Ferry promised her. "Listen, dear one. I have so much planned for us today. Come now. Up-up!"

He bent his knees a little so she could climb more easily into his saddle.

Cher lifted a finger and poked his cheek. "Is this a trick?" she said, standing her ground. "Are you finally going to eat me?"

"Now, we both know that isn't what you want."

"You're right. It isn't. But the deal—"

"The deal is off," said Ferry. "Remember? Now are you going to climb aboard, or do I have to go enjoy the surprise myself?"

She still didn't move. "This doesn't make any sense."

The sun flickered overhead, bright white and then gray and then suddenly white again, casting everything in a surreal glow. The river rose too, an extra inch or two of water lapping and churning around Cher's belly, before slowing to a leisurely current.

She blinked.

Ferry glitched, disappearing and reappearing.

"Something's wrong," she muttered to herself. She remembered so much blood, and the house...

"Nothing is wrong," said the kelpie.

That was all she needed to hear. All she wanted. Even if it wasn't the truth.

Cher hoisted herself up into the saddle. "What's this surprise then?" she asked.

"I'm not telling," Ferry teased.

"Oh, come on! Pretty, pretty please?"

The kelpie trod water and let the current carry them downriver. Cher prodded his side with her knee.

"Tell me!"

"Fine," he said. "We're going on a little afternoon whale-watching tour. And we may be meeting someone there."

"Who?"

Ferry didn't answer right away, and Cher poked him again.

"*Who?*"

"Oh, let's just say there are two friendly spirits who have been watching over you this whole time. They would like to finally steal some special bonding time with the daughter they're so proud of..."

She gasped. "Ferry!" she squealed and leaned forward to throw her arms around his neck.

A splash of the Crane River slipped its way down her throat. It tasted strange, like rust.

She sat back up, coughing up the water into her palm. A droplet of it curved down her wrist and around her forearm. It bore a reddish-purple tint.

The sun shone fiercer, and when she blinked again, the water cupped in her hand was as clear as ever.

"Everything okay?" Ferry asked her.

She shifted in the saddle. Déjà-vu tickled the back of her brain.

"Yeah," she said. "Of course. Everything's perfect. Exactly how it should be." She patted the back of his head, tangled her fingers into his mane, and decided she would never let go. "Thank you."

Charity turned her chin to the sun and shut her eyes against the light, letting it consume her. The warmth of those rays felt so real, in spite of everything.

She couldn't have asked for more.

The End

About Lee Ann Kostempski

Lee Ann Kostempski is a writer from the Buffalo, NY area, where she is also a librarian. In 2015, she graduated from Canisius College with a Bachelor's degree in English and Creative Writing, and in 2017 she received her Master's in Information and Library Science from the University at Buffalo. Her favorite thing to do is write dark, scary stories while she listens to disco, city pop, or K-pop, occasionally taking breaks to smother her two cats with love or play some video games with her partner. *The World As It Should Be* is her first novel.

Stay in the Know

Join the Mocha Memoirs monthly newsletter!

NOW!

Or visit
https://mochamemoirspress.com/newsletter

Other Stories You May Enjoy

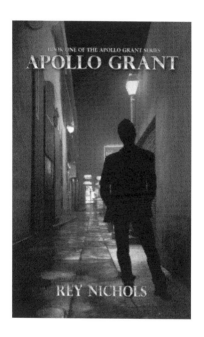

THE
BLACK
HOLE

"The Black Hole is a pulse-pounding page-turner a real life
nightmare." – Midwest Book Review

L. MARIE WOOD

Made in the USA
Columbia, SC
05 October 2023

23889263R00139